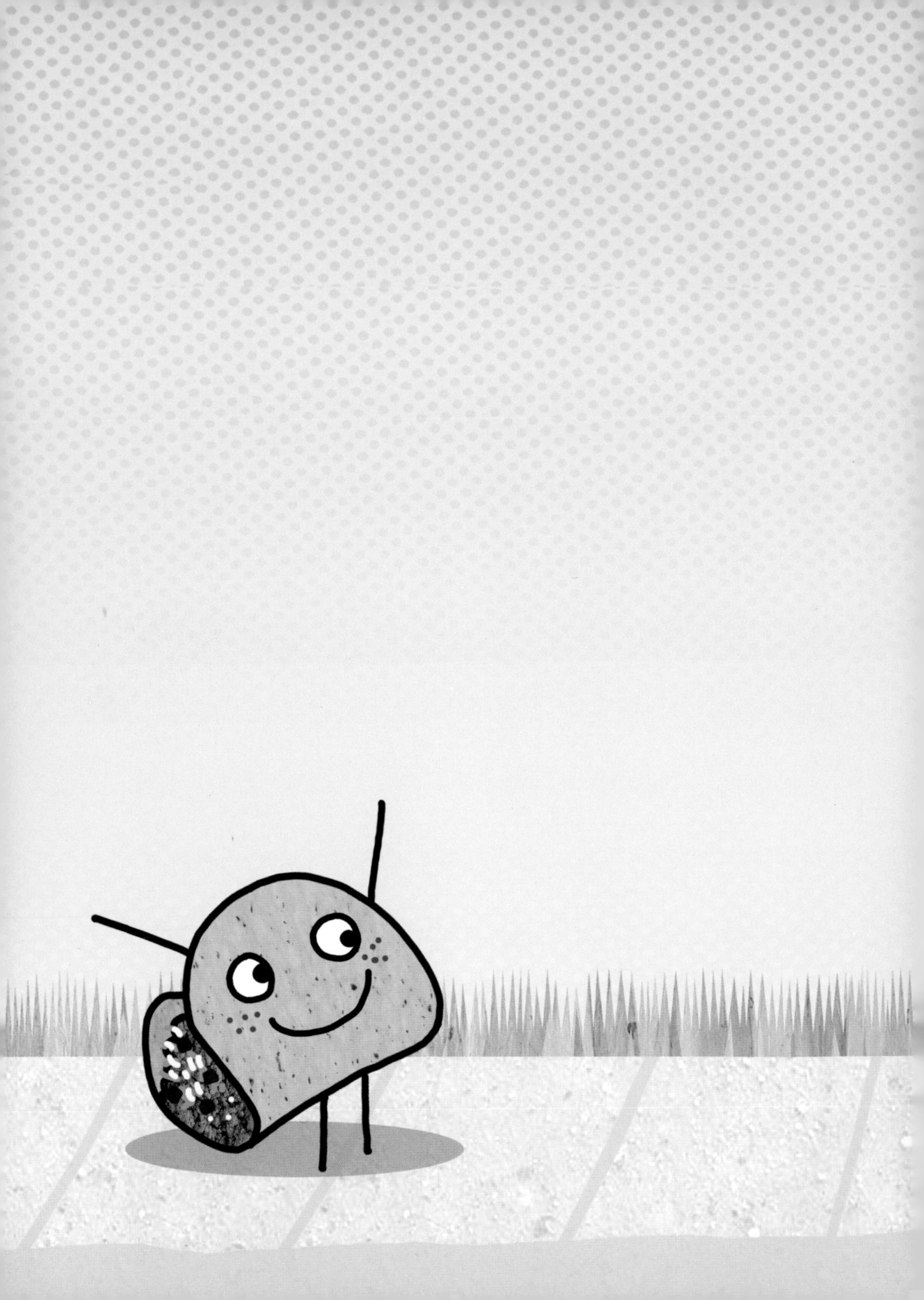

Pizza and Taco

WHO'S THE BEST?

STEPHEN SHASKAN

A STEPPING STONE BOOK™

Random House 🏠 New York

To all the pizzas and tacos I've loved

Copyright © 2020 by Stephen Shaskan
All rights reserved. Published in the United States by Random House Children's Books,
a division of Penguin Random House LLC, New York.
Random House and the colophon are registered trademarks and A Stepping Stone Book
and the colophon are trademarks of Penguin Random House LLC.
Visit us on the Web! rhcbooks.com
Educators and librarians, for a variety of teaching tools, visit us at RHTeachersLibrarians.com

Library of Congress Cataloging-in-Publication Data
Names: Shaskan, Stephen, author, illustrator.
Title: Pizza and Taco : who's the best? / Stephen Shaskan.
Other titles: Pizza and Taco, who is the best?
Description: First edition. | New York : Random House Children's Books,
[2020] | Audience: Ages 5–8. | Audience: Grades 2–3.
Summary: Best friends Pizza and Taco agree on nearly everything until Pizza declares
himself the best of all, leading to debating, voting, competing, and finally defining what being
the best really means.
Identifiers: LCCN 2019031107 (print) | LCCN 2019031108 (ebook)
ISBN 978-0-593-12330-0 (hardcover) | ISBN 978-0-593-12331-7 (library binding)
ISBN 978-0-593-12332-4 (ebook)
Subjects: CYAC: Best friends—Fiction. | Friendship—Fiction. | Pizza—Fiction.
Tacos—Fiction. | Contests—Fiction.
Classification: LCC PZ7.S532418 Piz 2020 (print) | LCC PZ7.S532418 (ebook) | DDC [E]—dc23

MANUFACTURED IN CHINA
10 9 8 7 6 5 4 3 2 1
First Edition
Random House Children's Books supports the First Amendment
and celebrates the right to read.

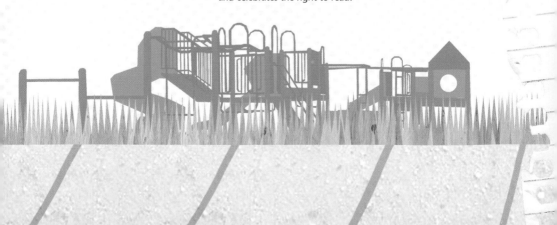

Contents

Chapter 1
PIZZA and TACO Are Best Friends

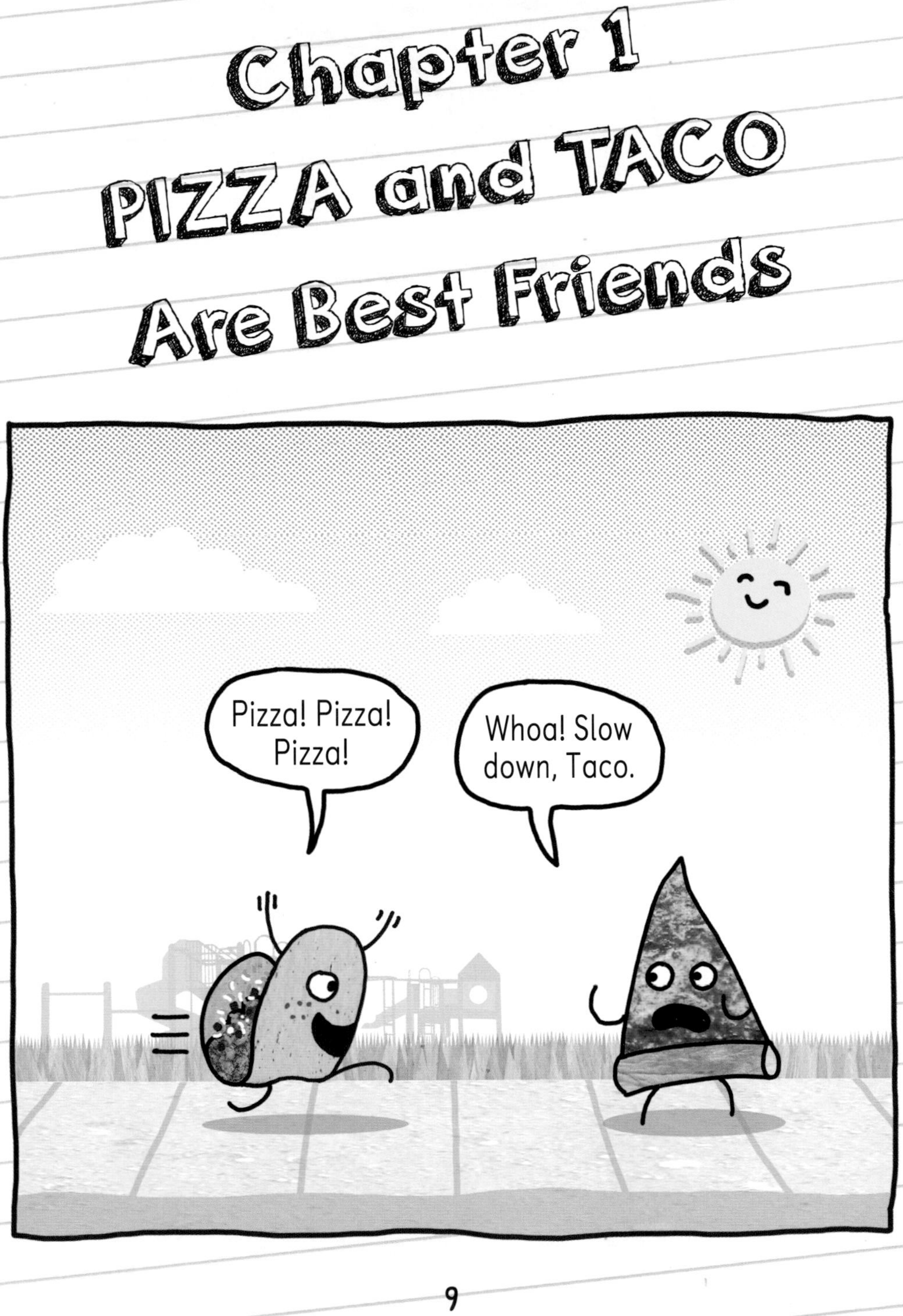

Pizza! Pizza! Pizza!
Whoa! Slow down, Taco.

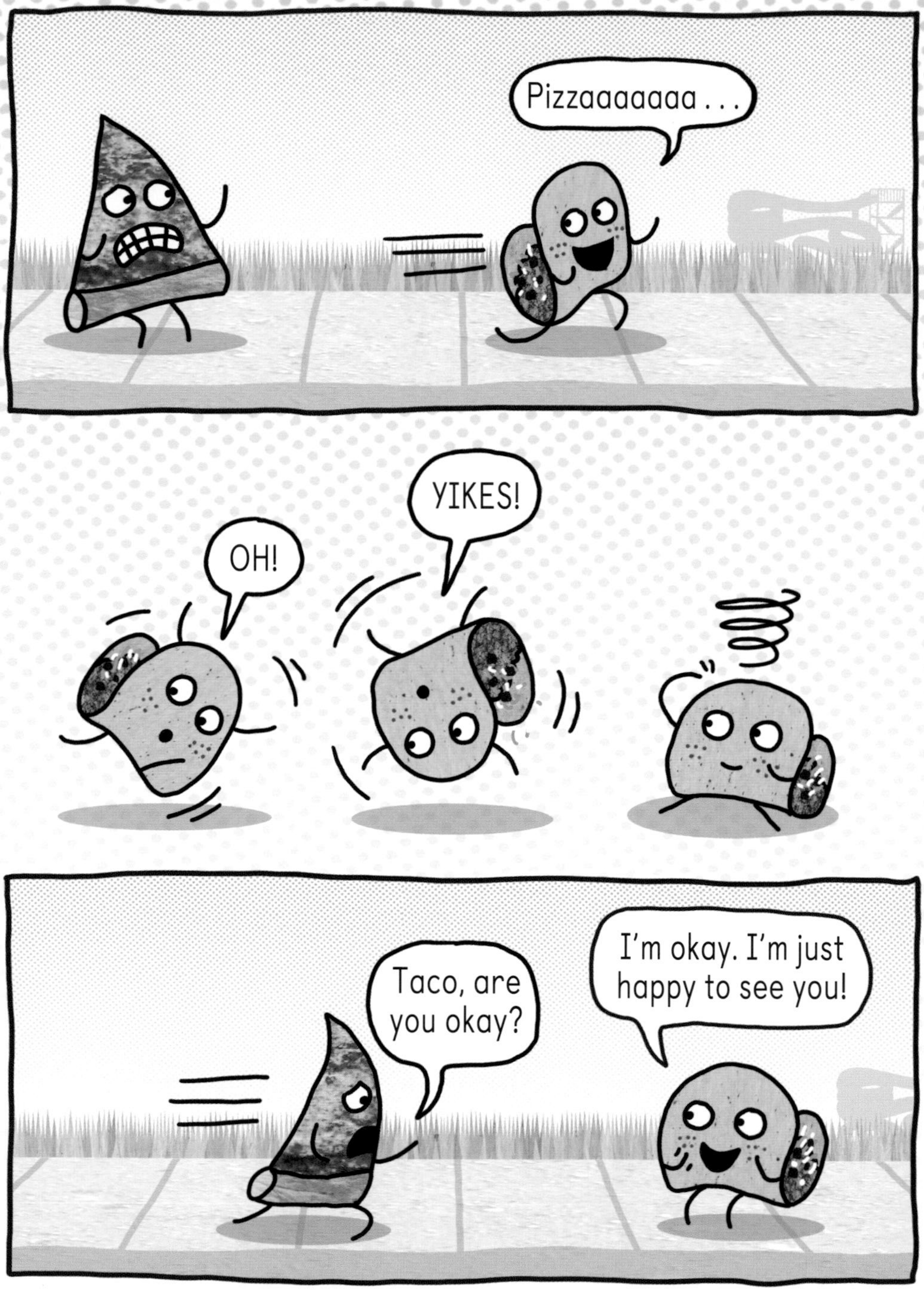
Pizzaaaaaaa . . .
OH!
YIKES!
Taco, are you okay?
I'm okay. I'm just happy to see you!

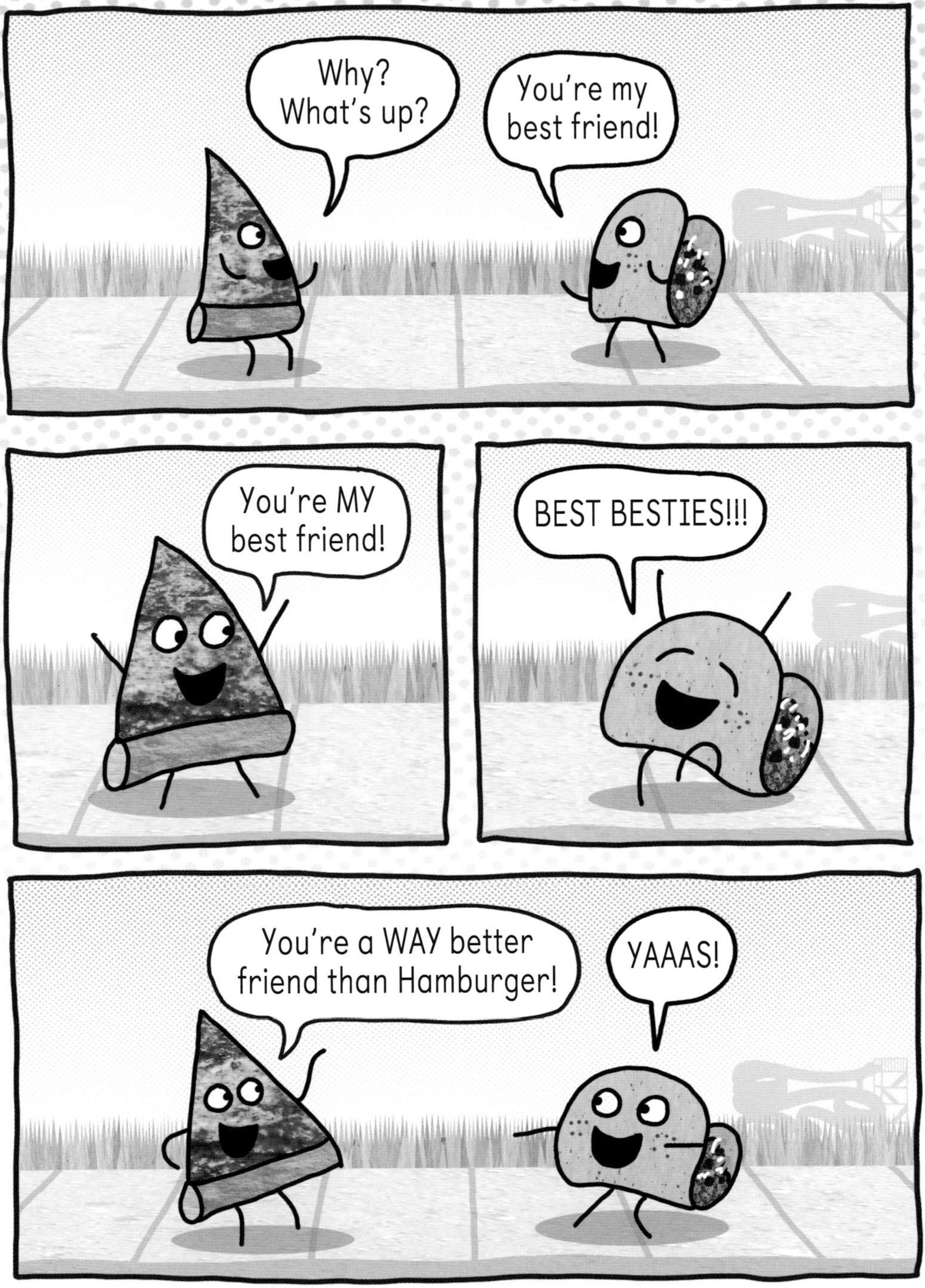
Why? What's up?
You're my best friend!
You're MY best friend!
BEST BESTIES!!!
You're a WAY better friend than Hamburger!
YAAAS!

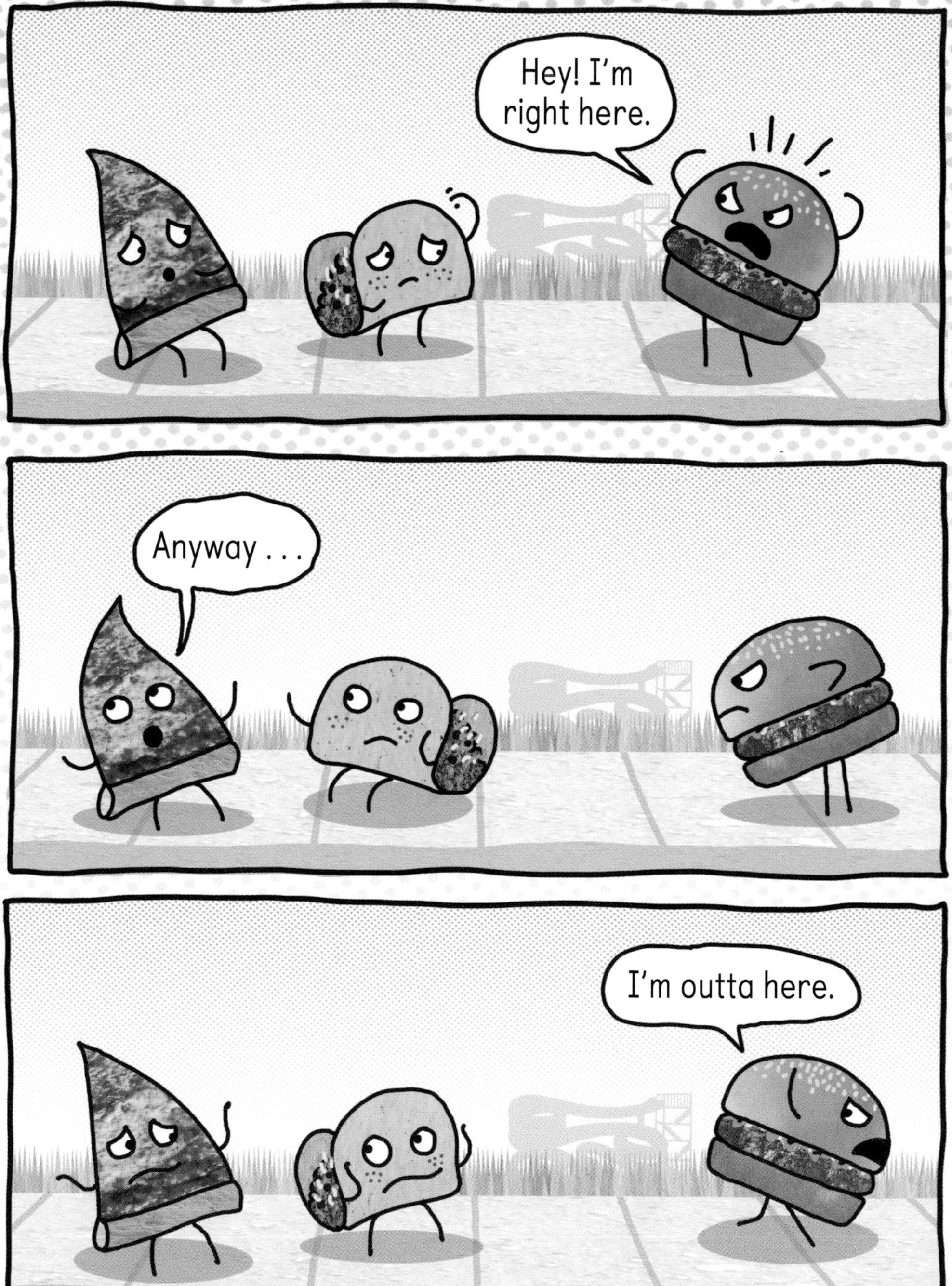
Hey! I'm right here.
Anyway . . .
I'm outta here.

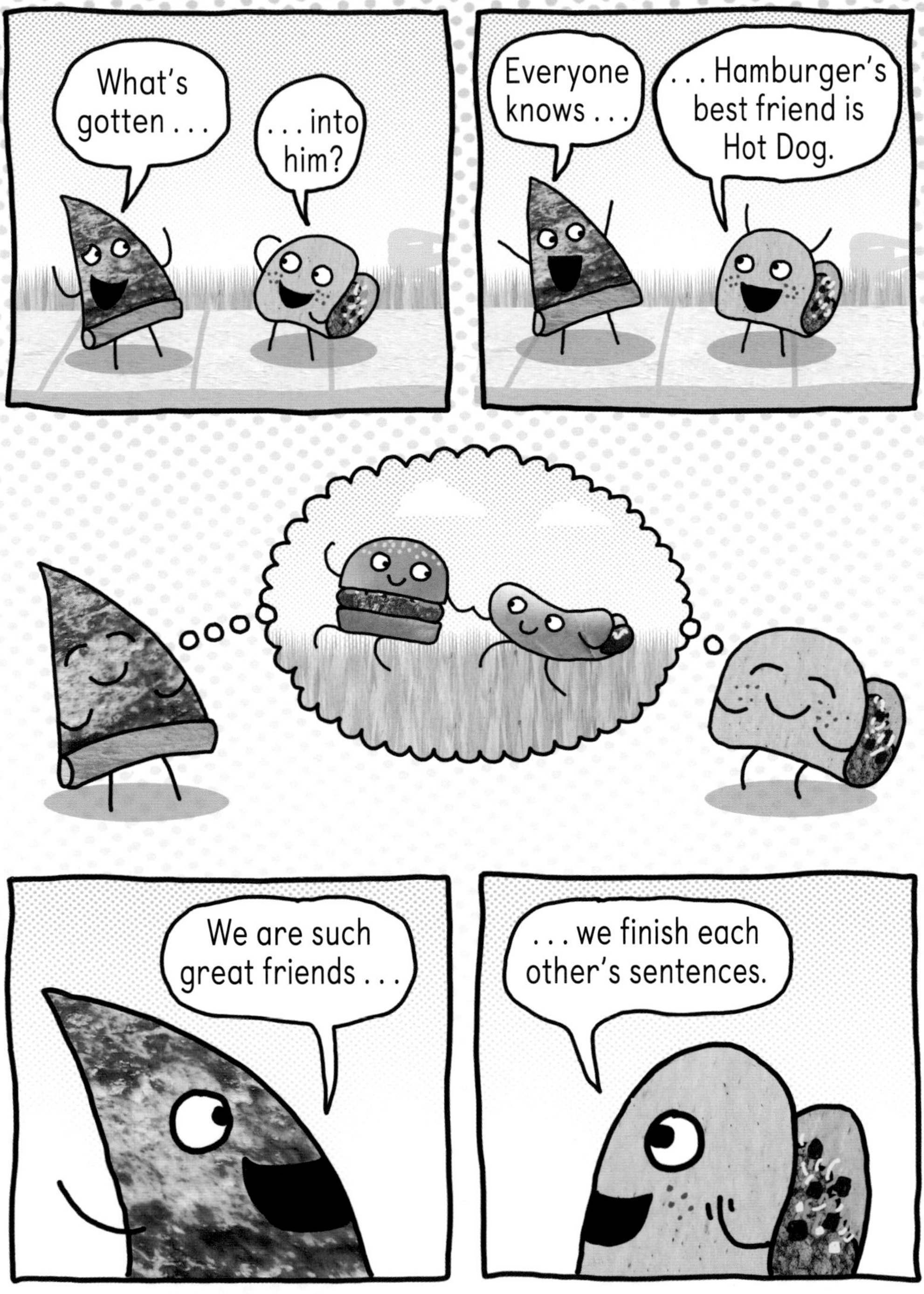
What's gotten . . .
. . . into him?
Everyone knows . . .
. . . Hamburger's best friend is Hot Dog.
We are such great friends . . .
. . . we finish each other's sentences.

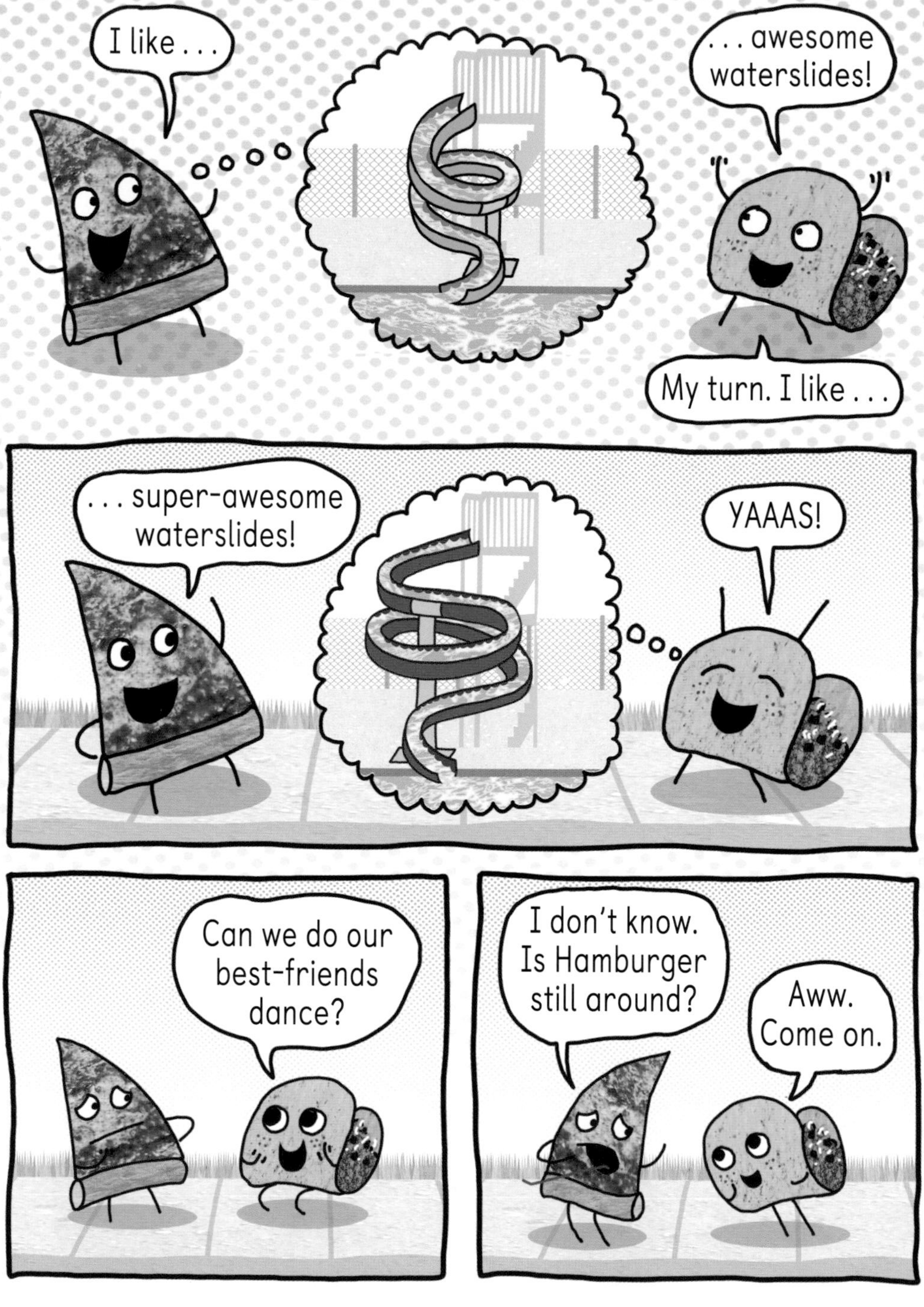
I like . . .
. . . awesome waterslides!
My turn. I like . . .
. . . super-awesome waterslides!
YAAAS!
Can we do our best-friends dance?
I don't know. Is Hamburger still around?
Aww. Come on.

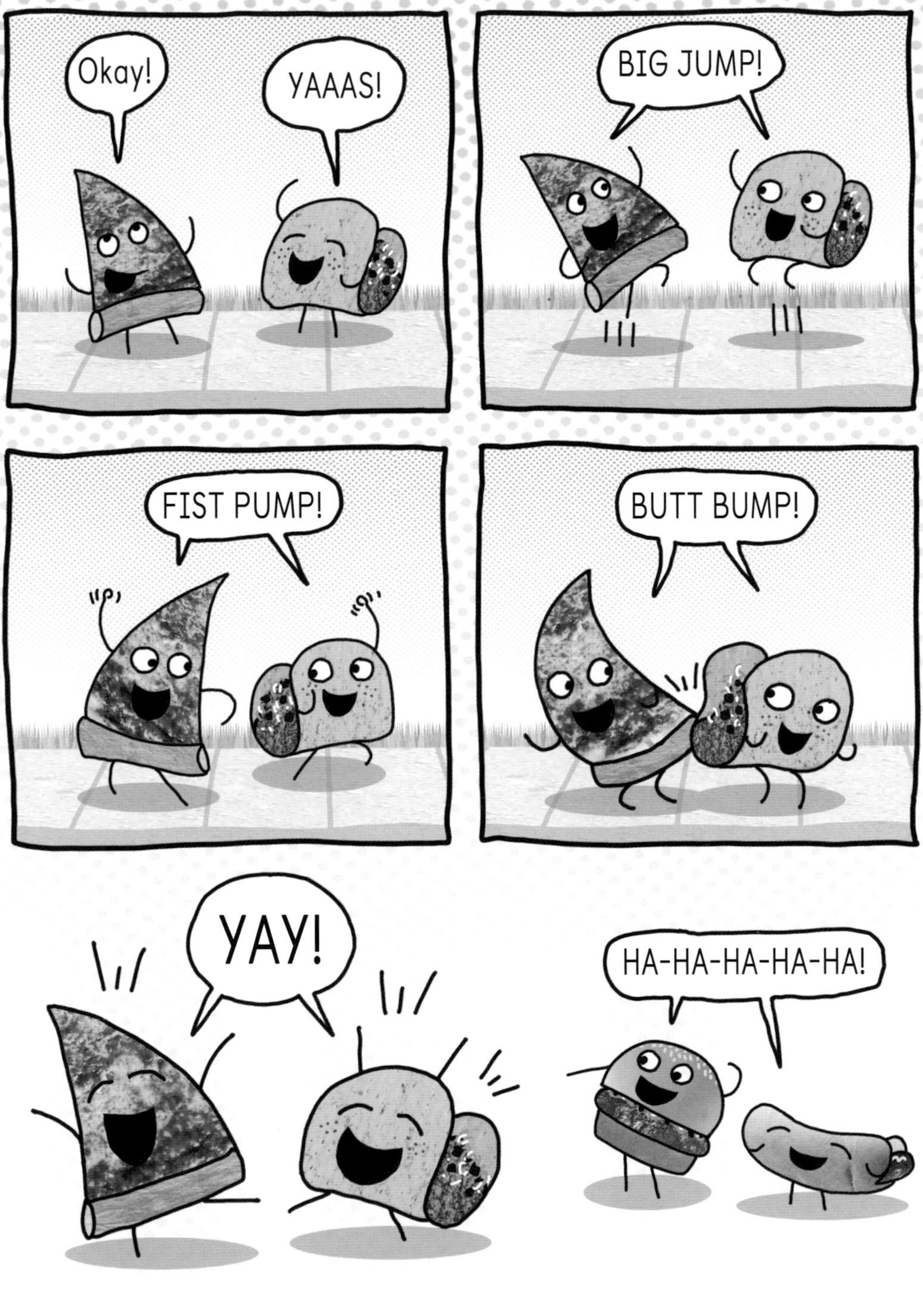
Okay!
YAAAS!
BIG JUMP!
FIST PUMP!
BUTT BUMP!
YAY!
HA-HA-HA-HA-HA!

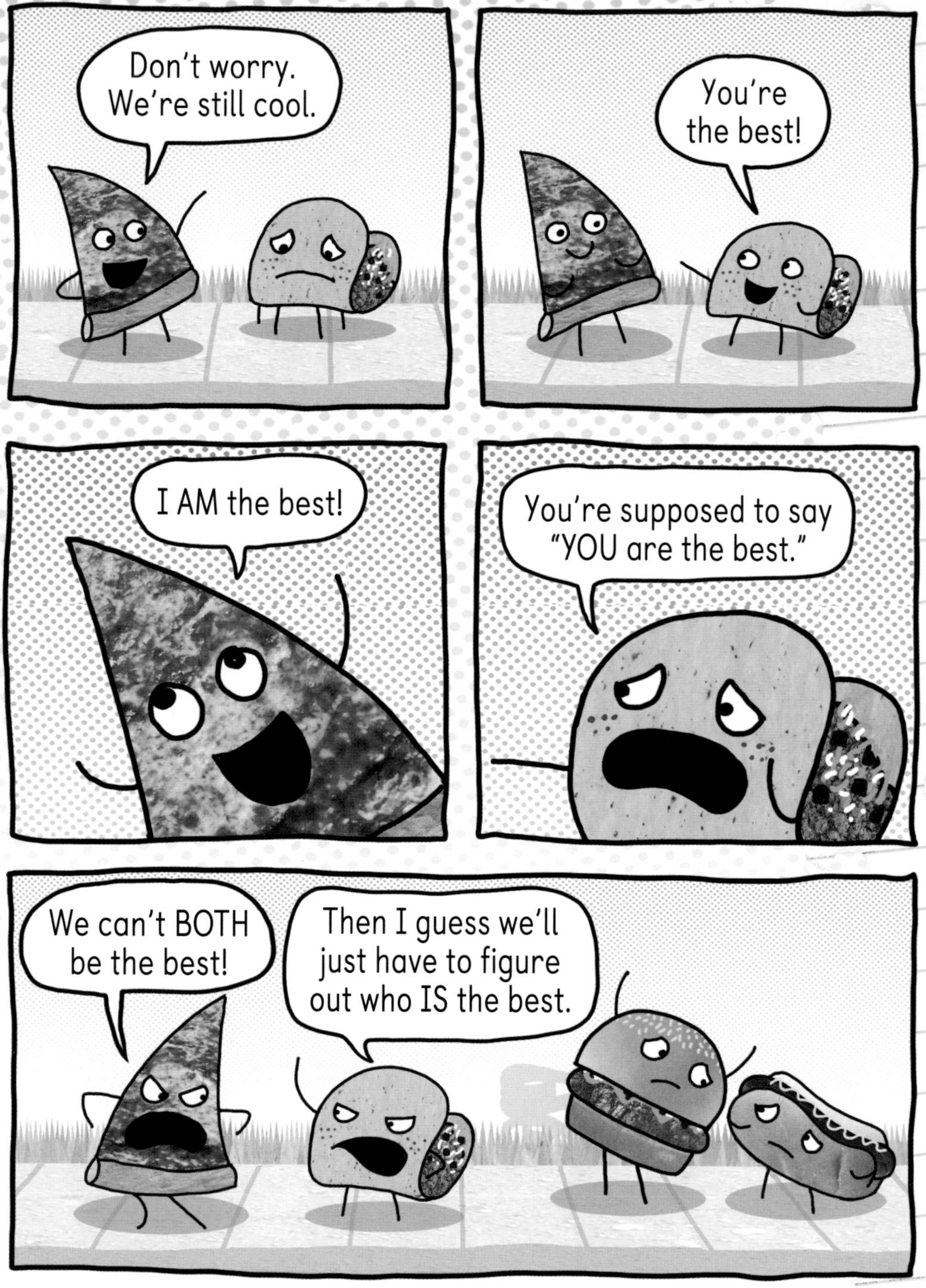
Don't worry. We're still cool.
You're the best!
I AM the best!
You're supposed to say "YOU are the best."
We can't BOTH be the best!
Then I guess we'll just have to figure out who IS the best.

Chapter 2
PIZZA and TACO: Who's the Best?

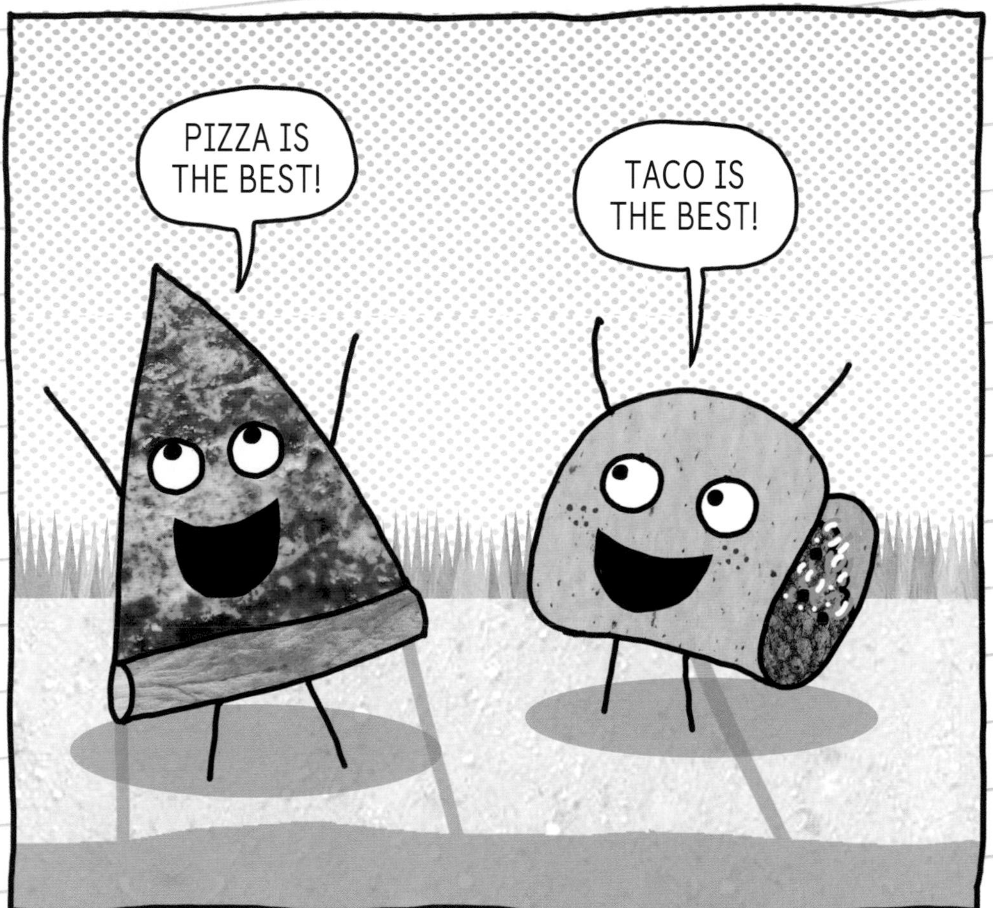
PIZZA IS THE BEST!
TACO IS THE BEST!

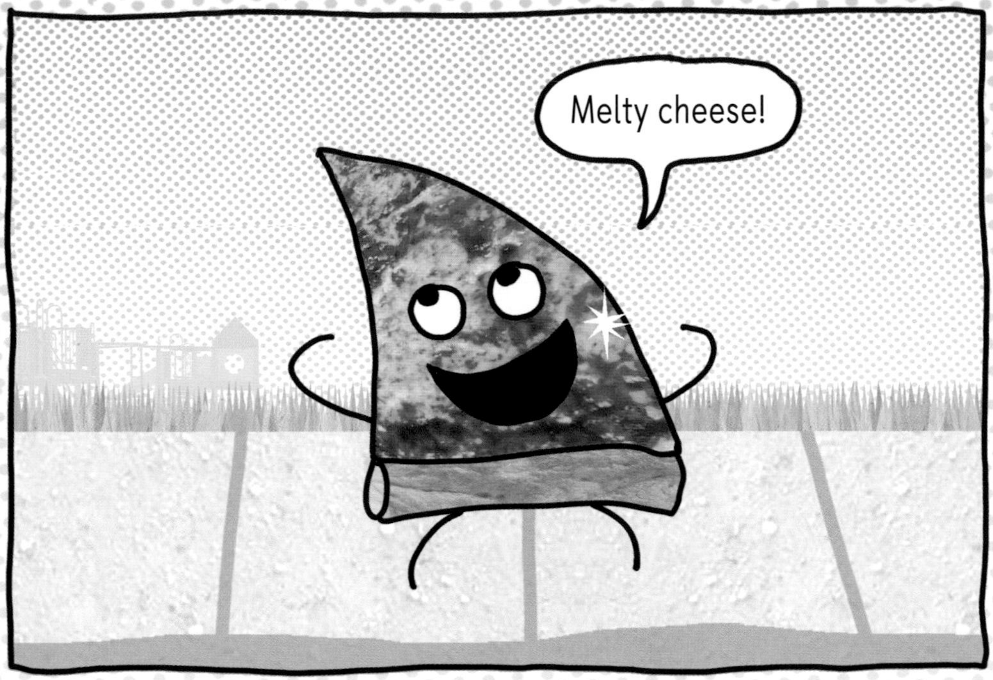
Melty cheese!

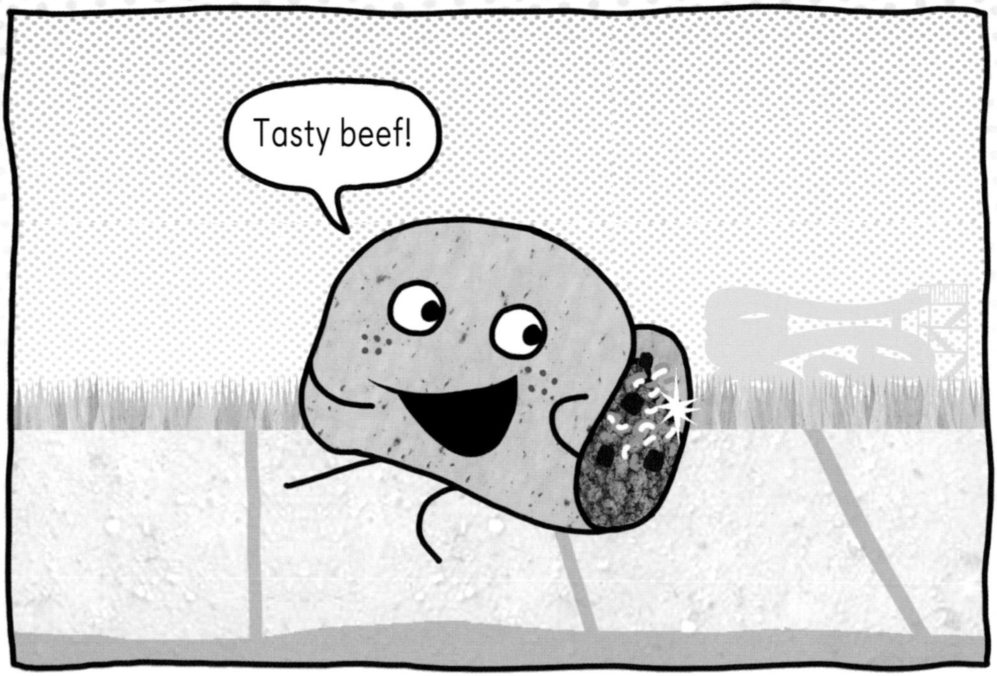
Tasty beef!

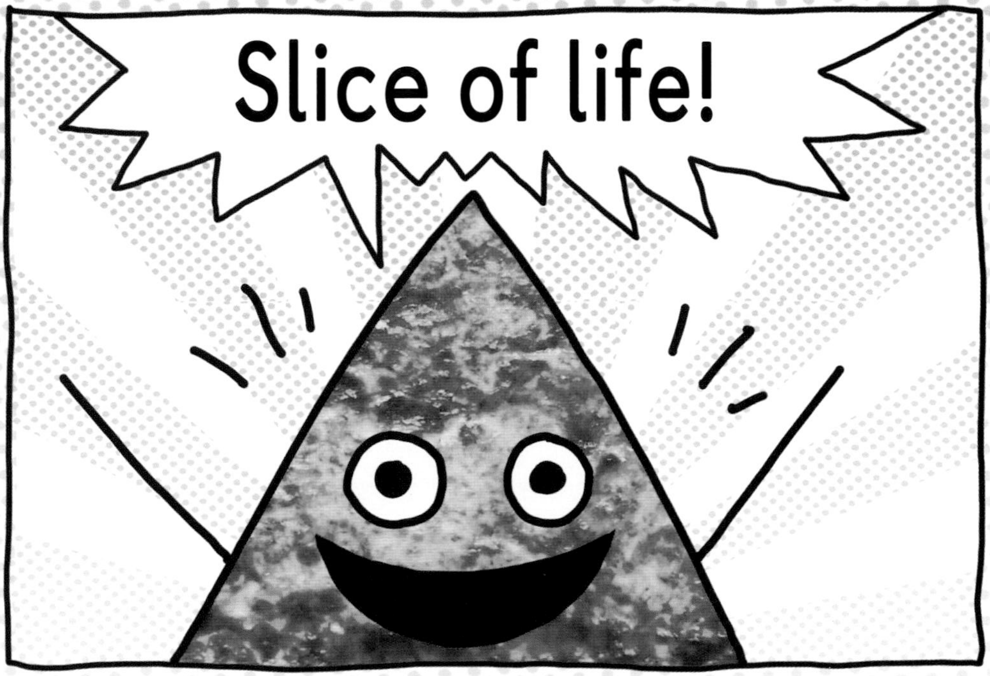
Slice of life!

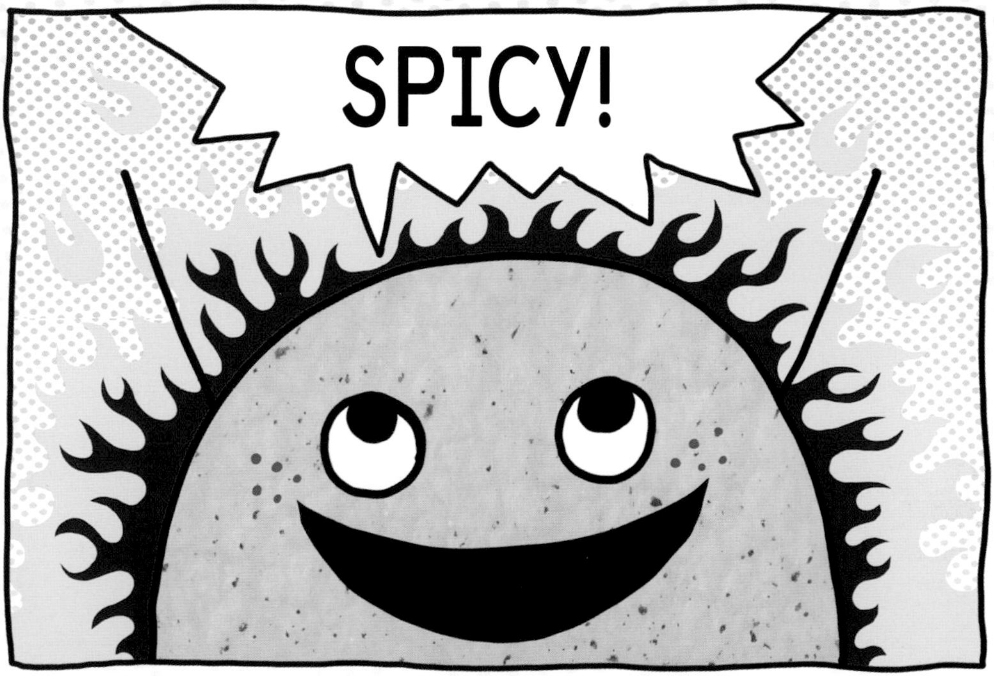
SPICY!

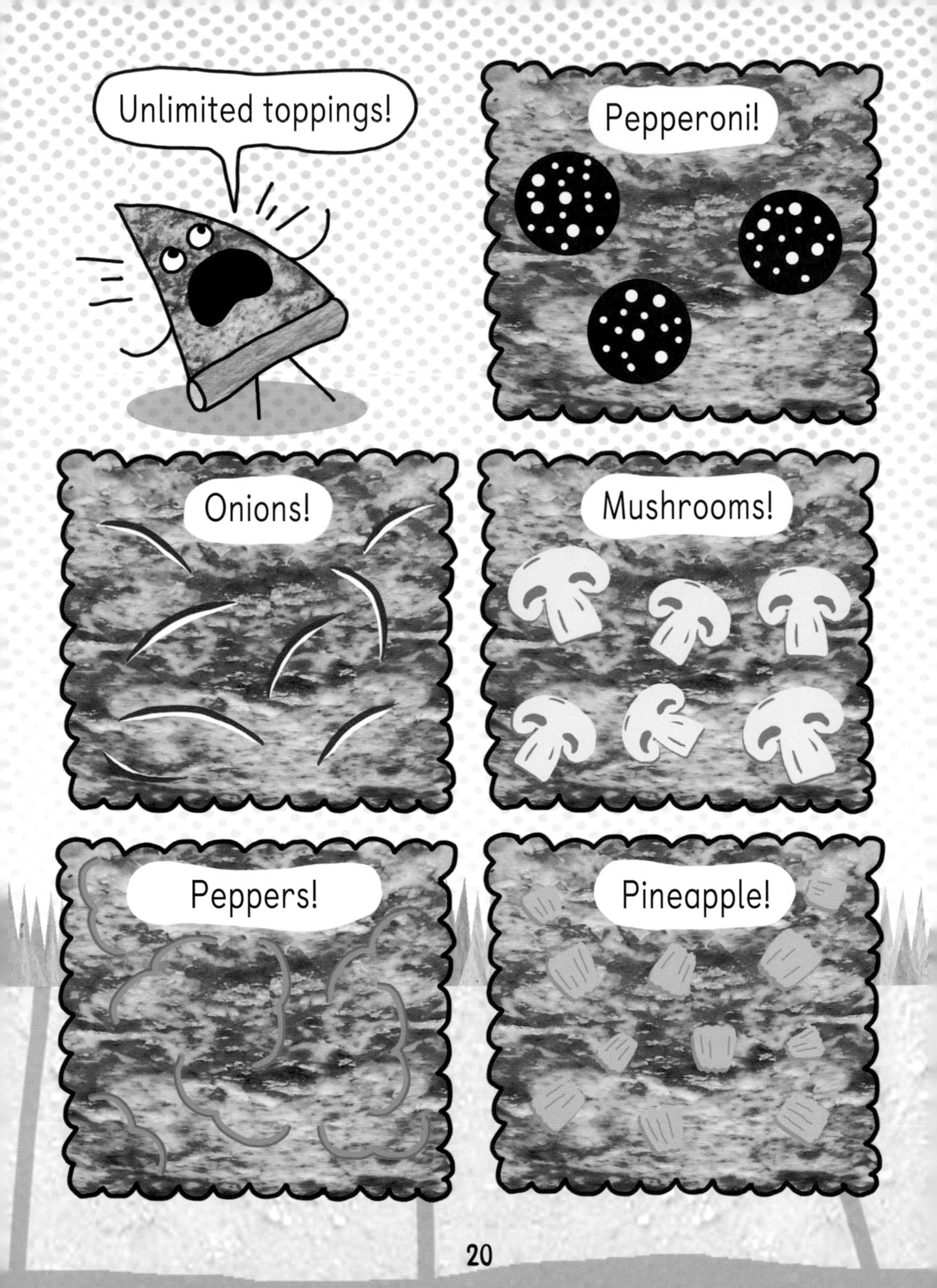
Unlimited toppings!
Pepperoni!
Onions!
Mushrooms!
Peppers!
Pineapple!

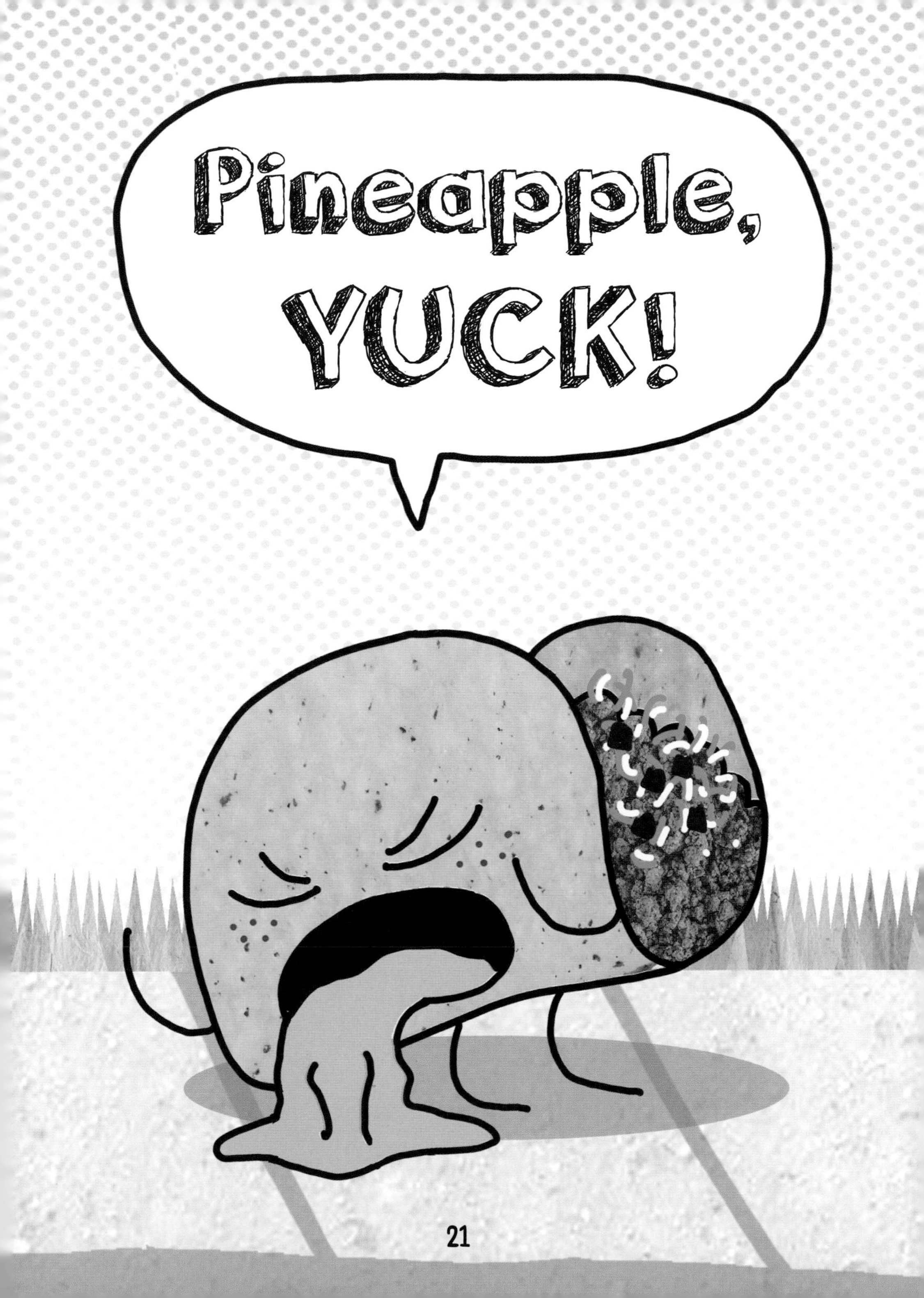
Pineapple, YUCK!

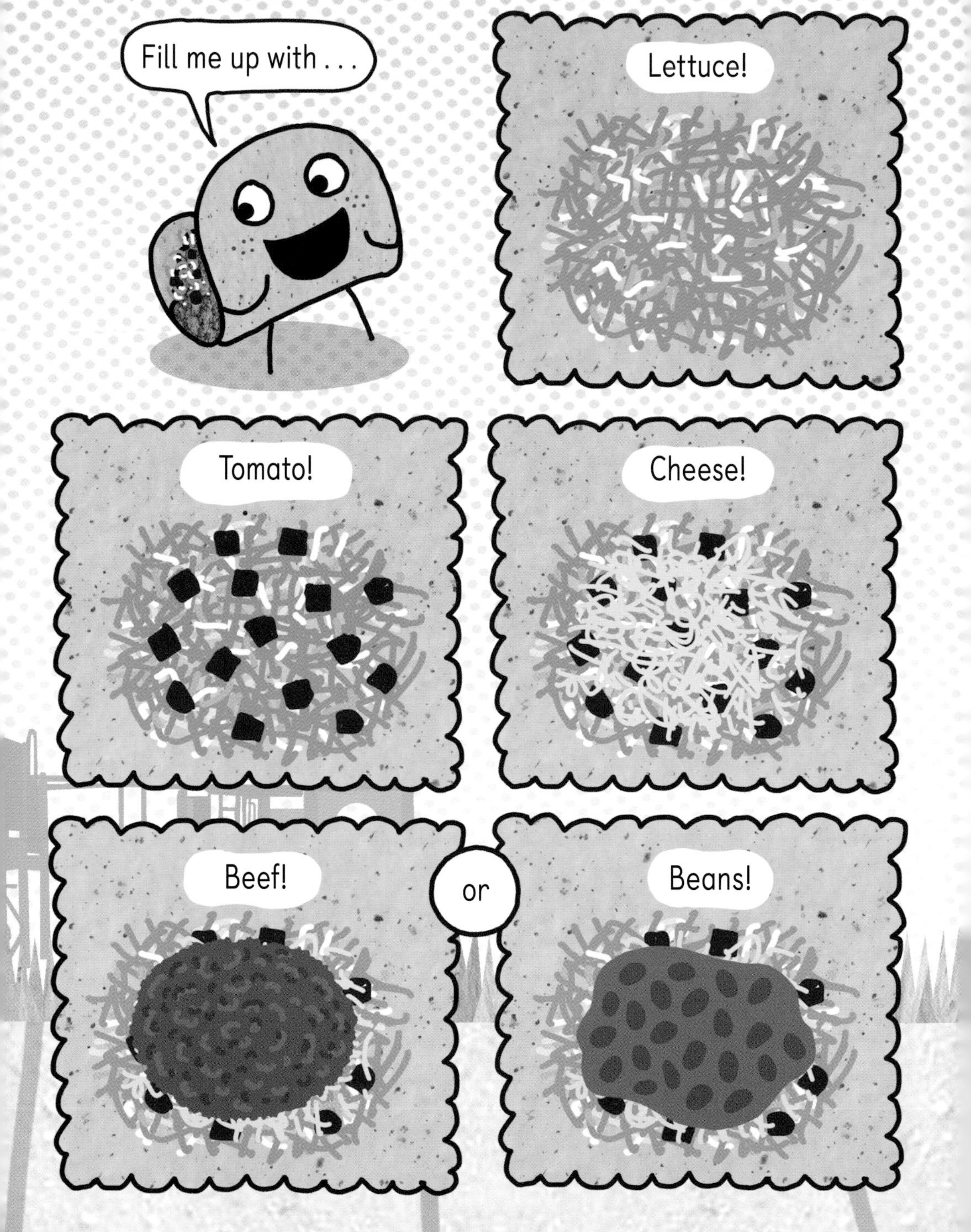
Fill me up with . . .
Lettuce!
Tomato!
Cheese!
Beef!
or
Beans!

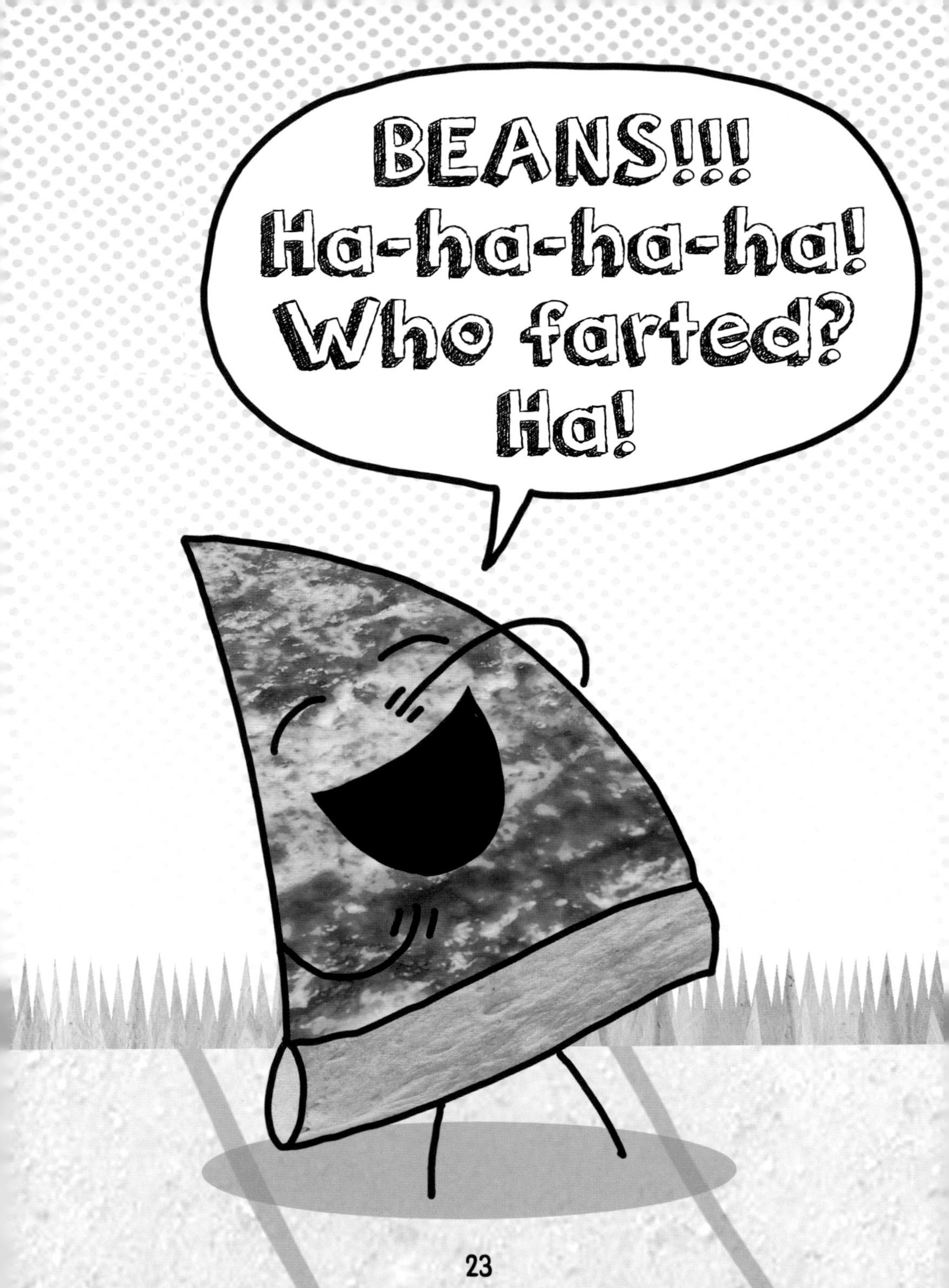
BEANS!!!
Ha-ha-ha-ha!
Who farted?
Ha!

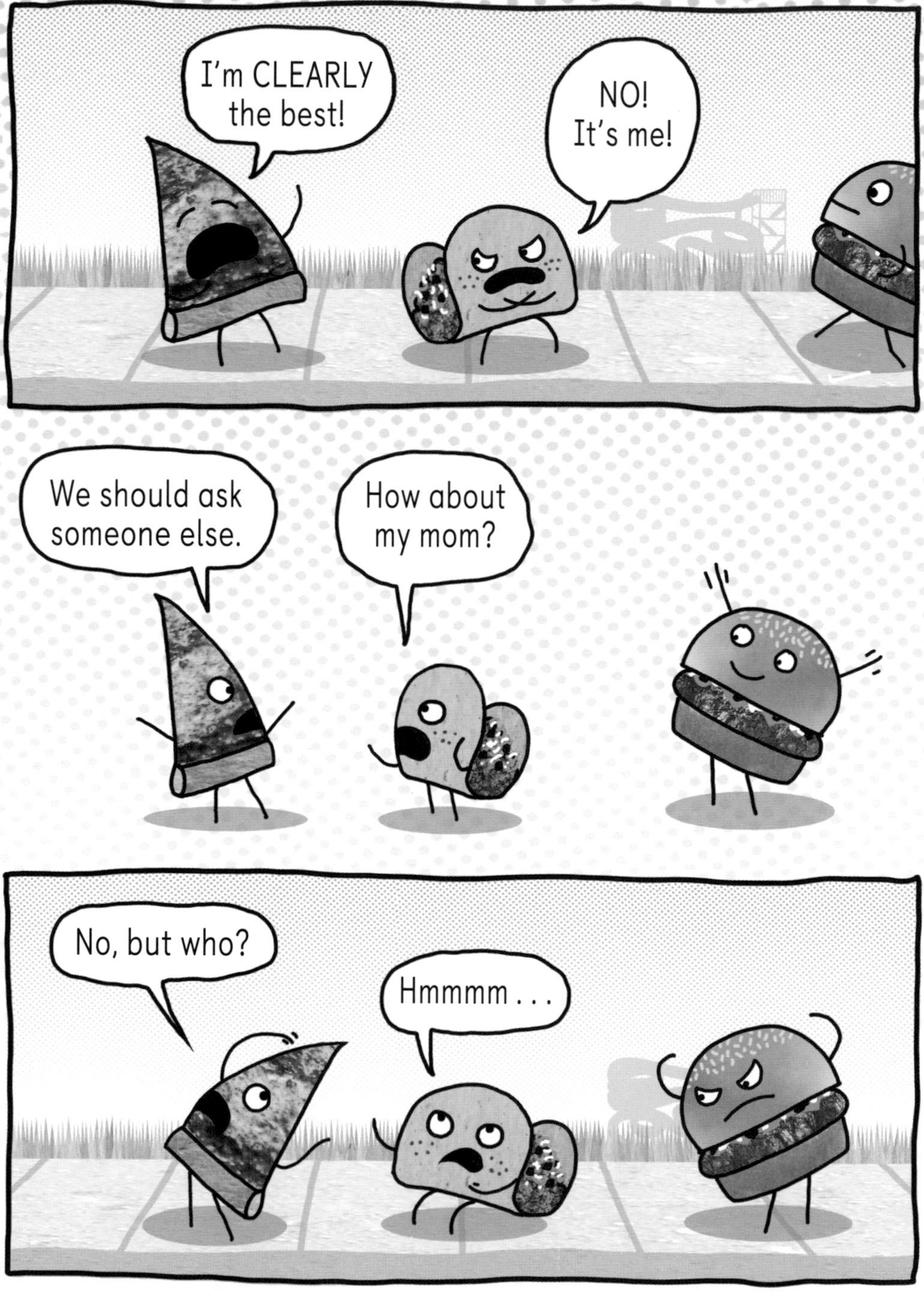
I'm CLEARLY the best!
NO! It's me!
We should ask someone else.
How about my mom?
No, but who?
Hmmmm . . .

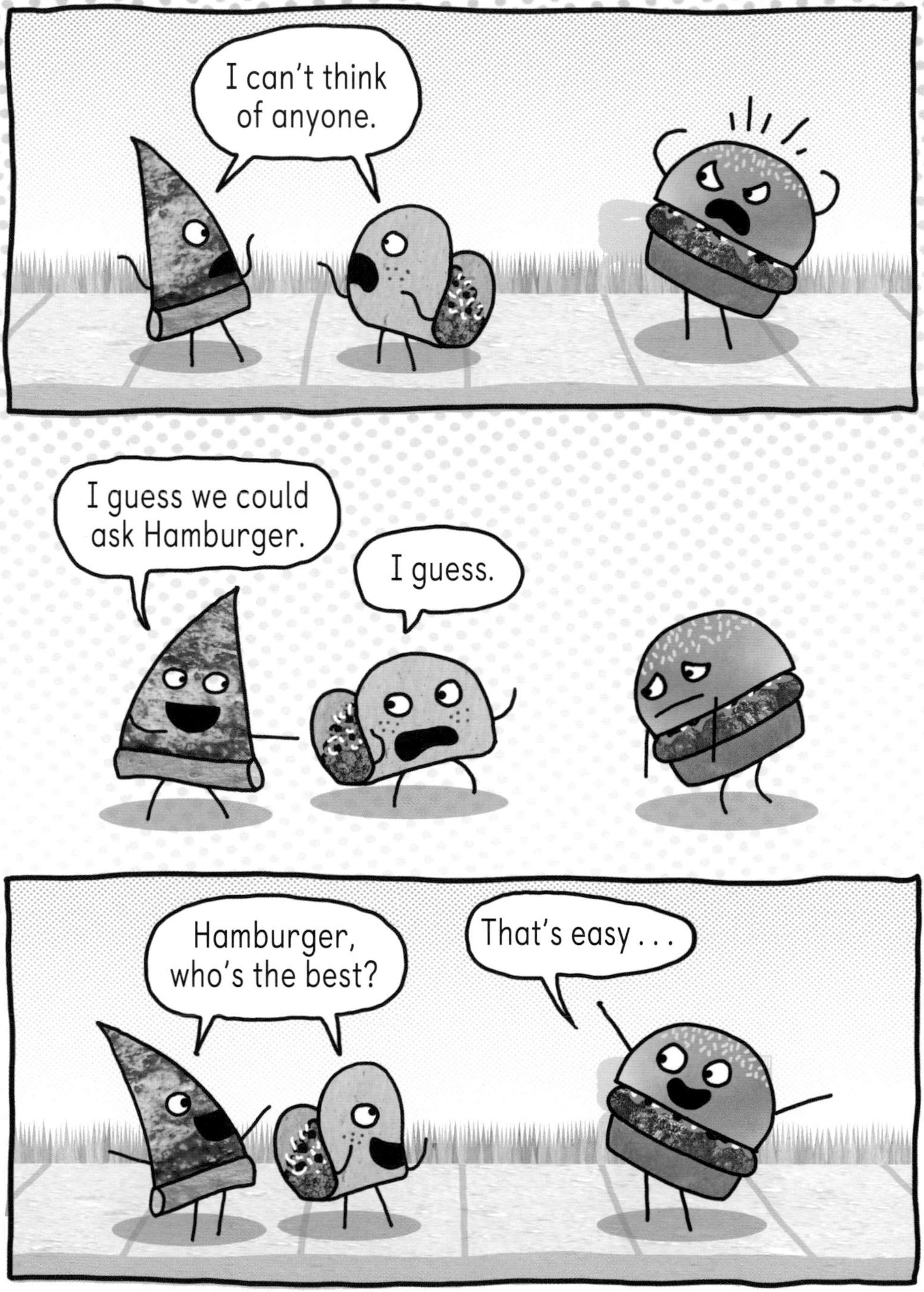
I can't think of anyone.
I guess we could ask Hamburger.
I guess.
Hamburger, who's the best?
That's easy . . .

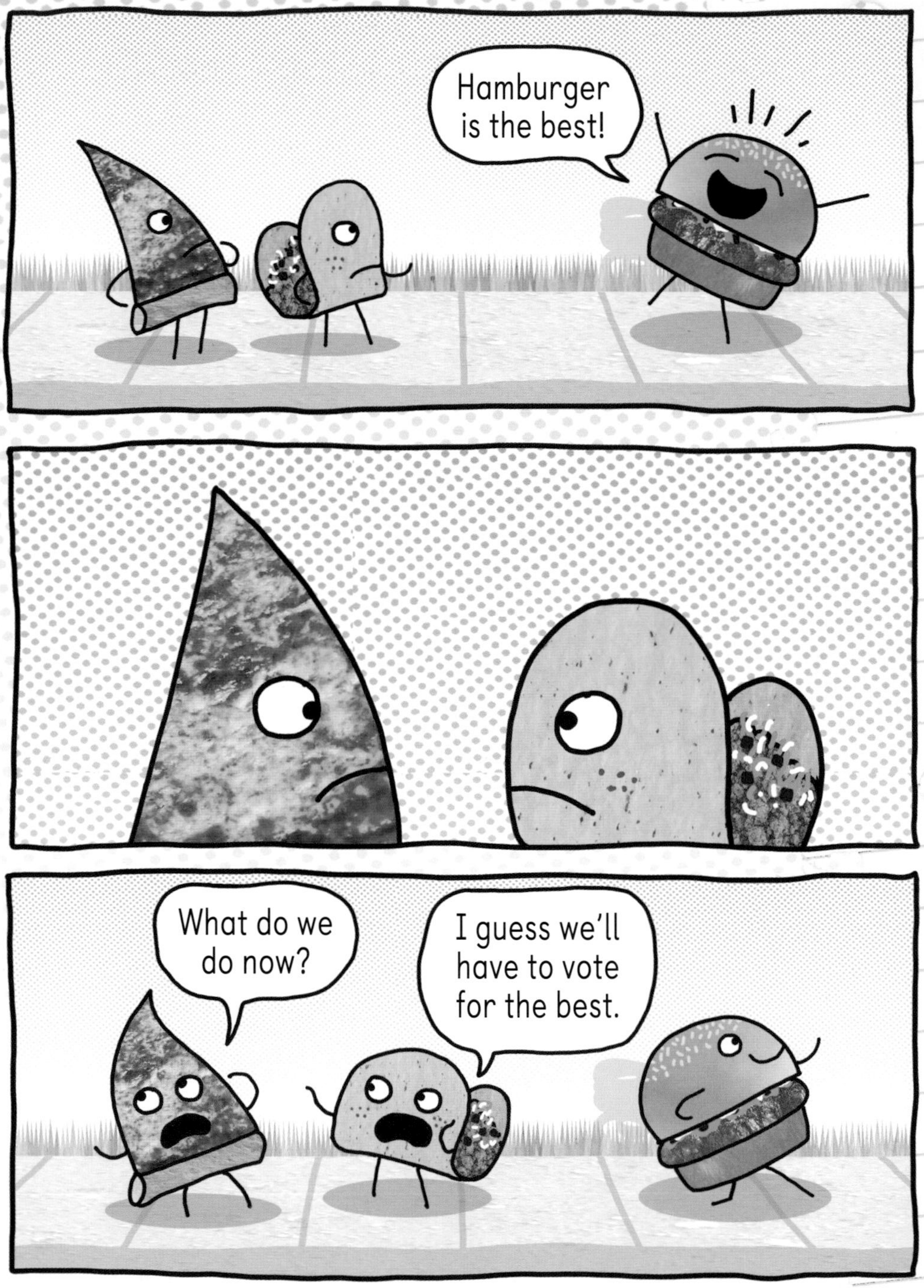
Hamburger is the best!
What do we do now?
I guess we'll have to vote for the best.

Chapter 3
PIZZA and TACO Vote for the Best!

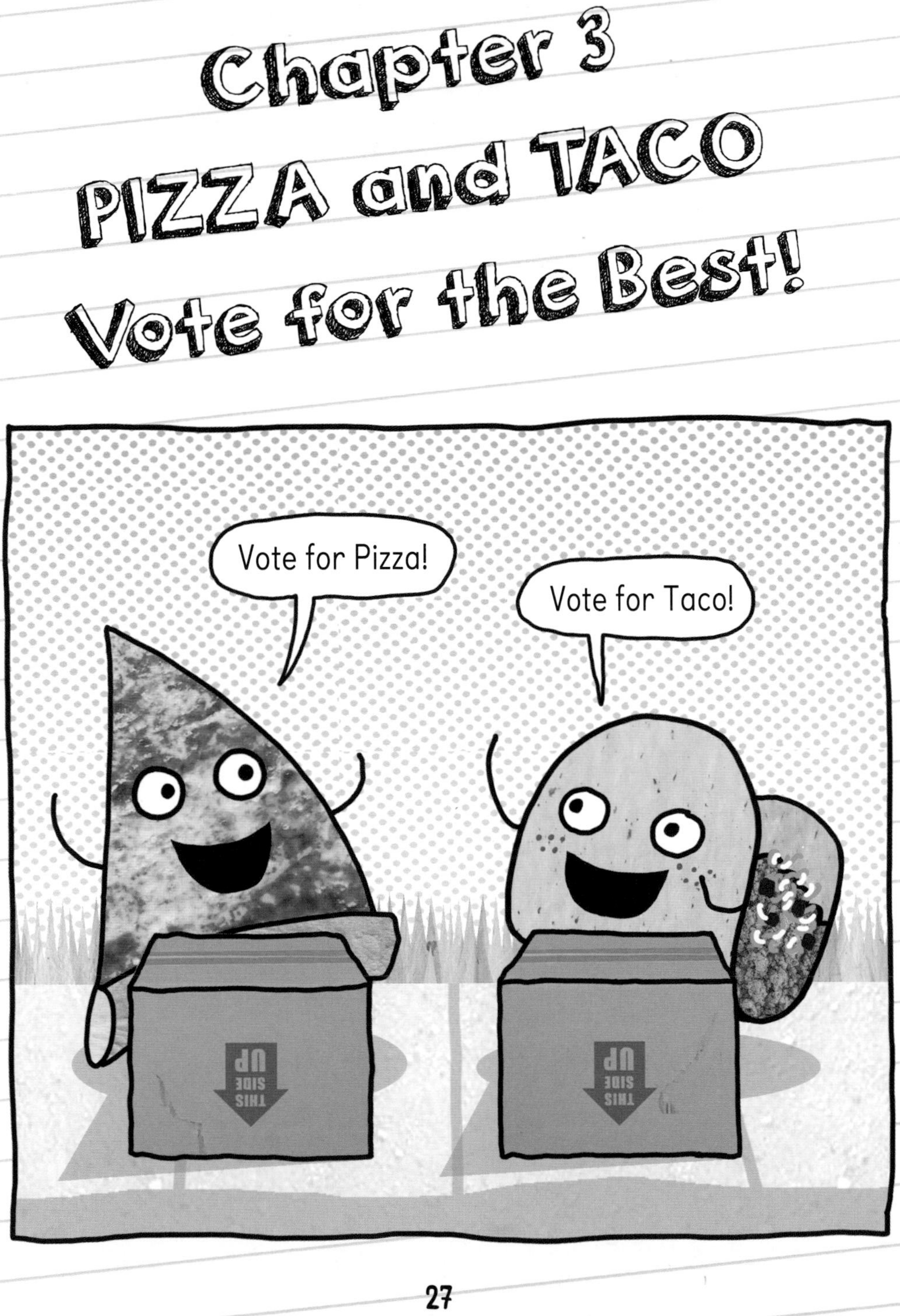

Vote for Pizza!
Vote for Taco!
THIS SIDE UP
THIS SIDE UP

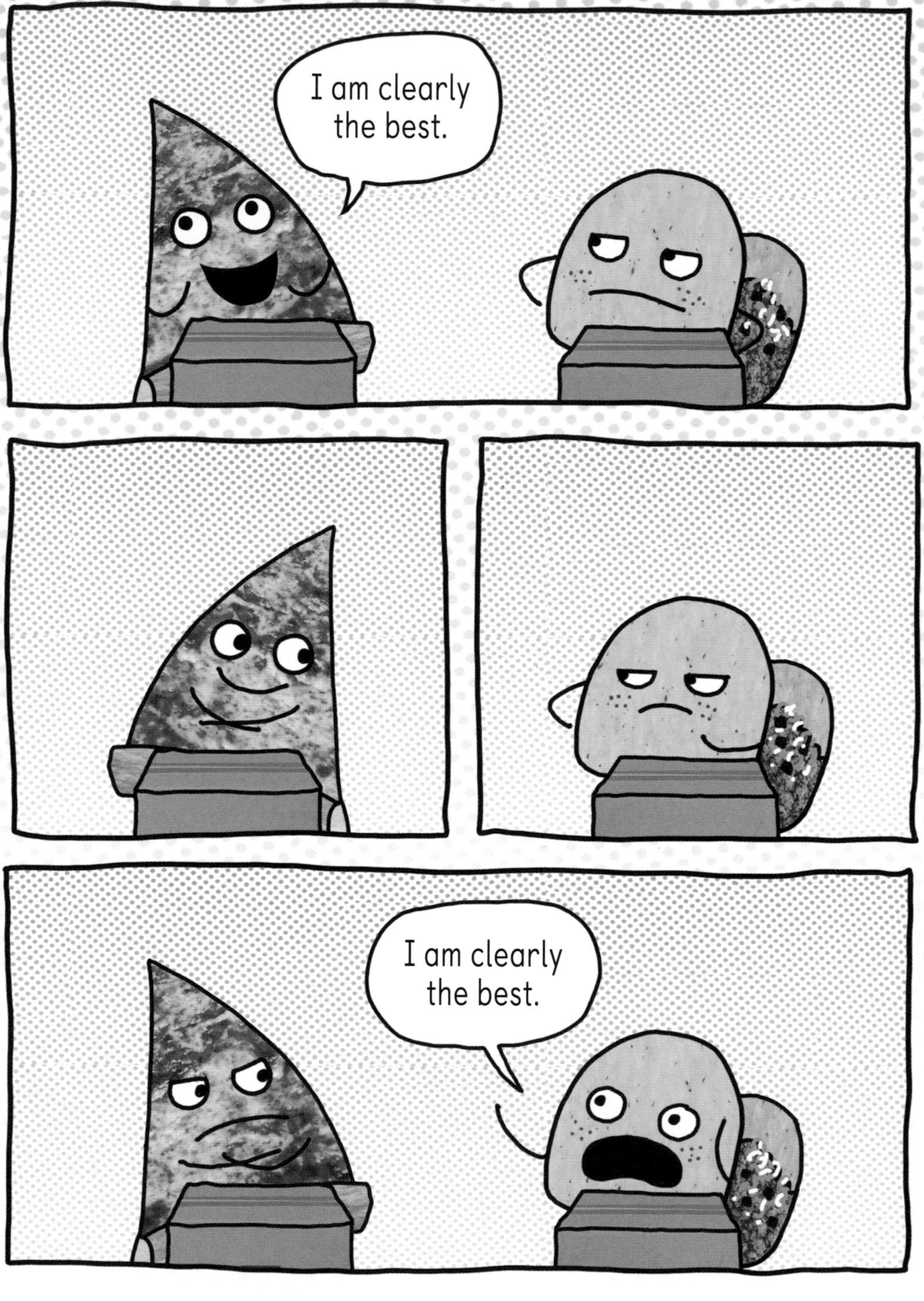
I am clearly the best.
I am clearly the best.

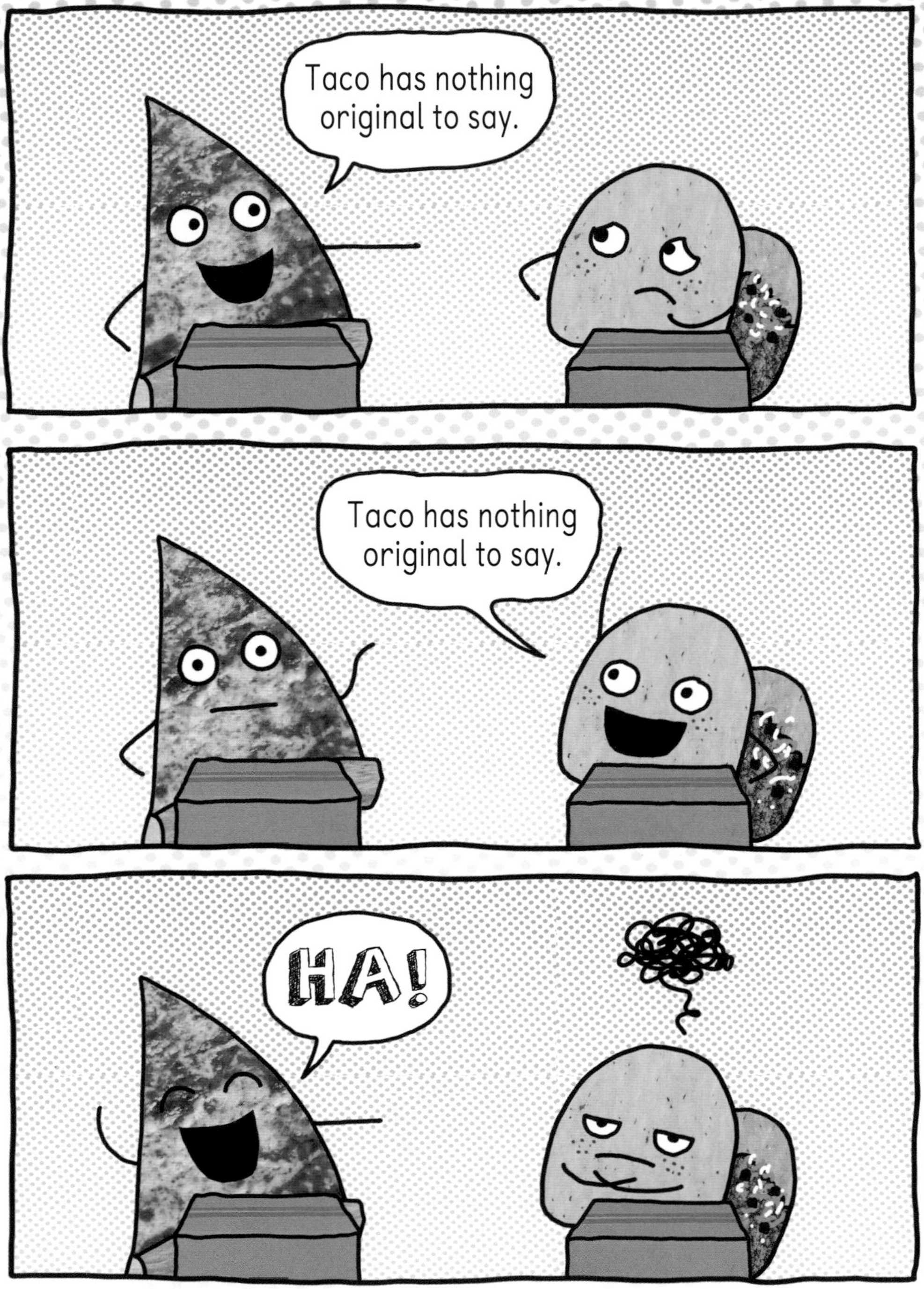
Taco has nothing original to say.
Taco has nothing original to say.
HA!

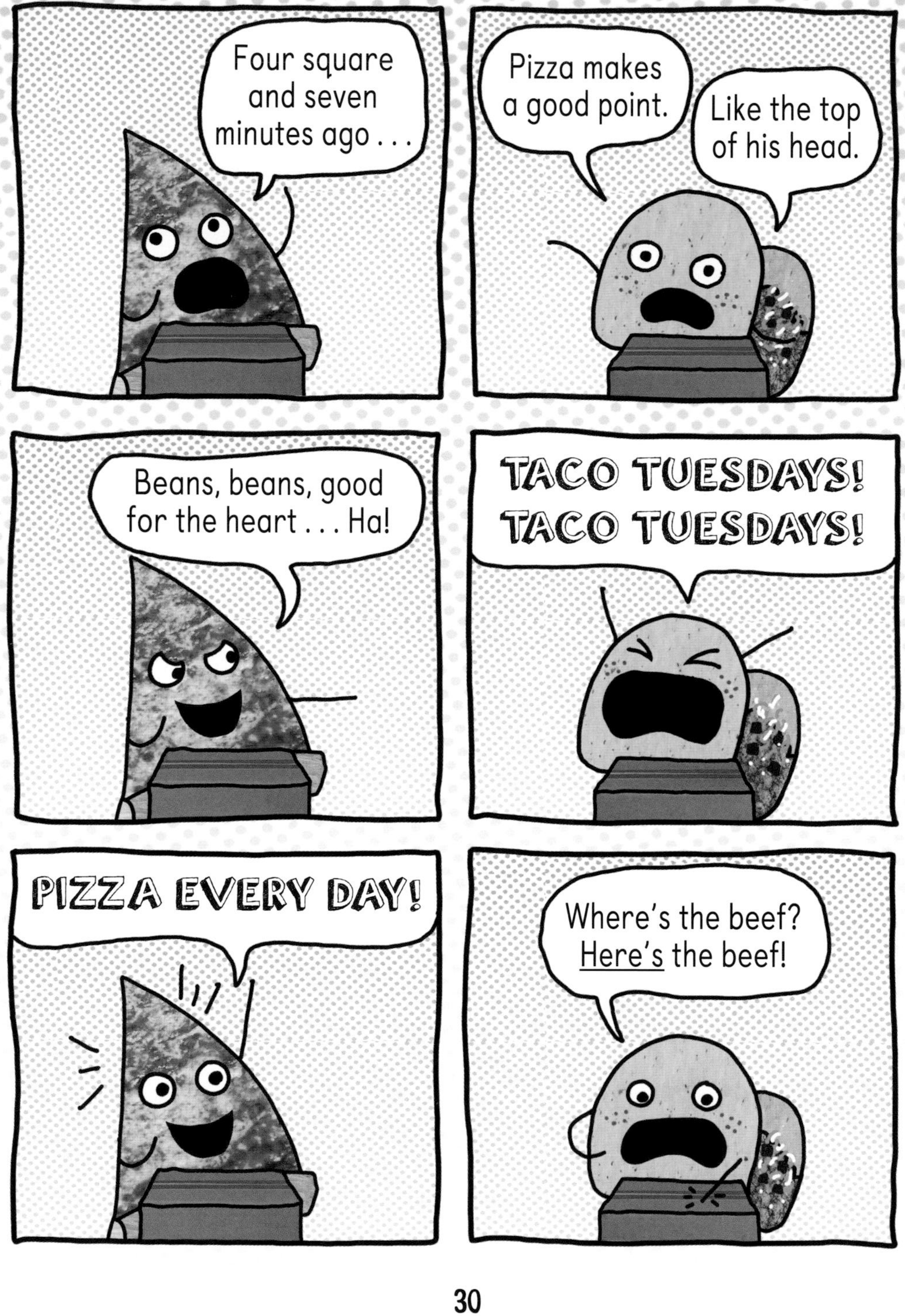
Four square and seven minutes ago . . .
Pizza makes a good point.
Like the top of his head.
Beans, beans, good for the heart . . . Ha!
TACO TUESDAYS! TACO TUESDAYS!
PIZZA EVERY DAY!
Where's the beef? Here's the beef!

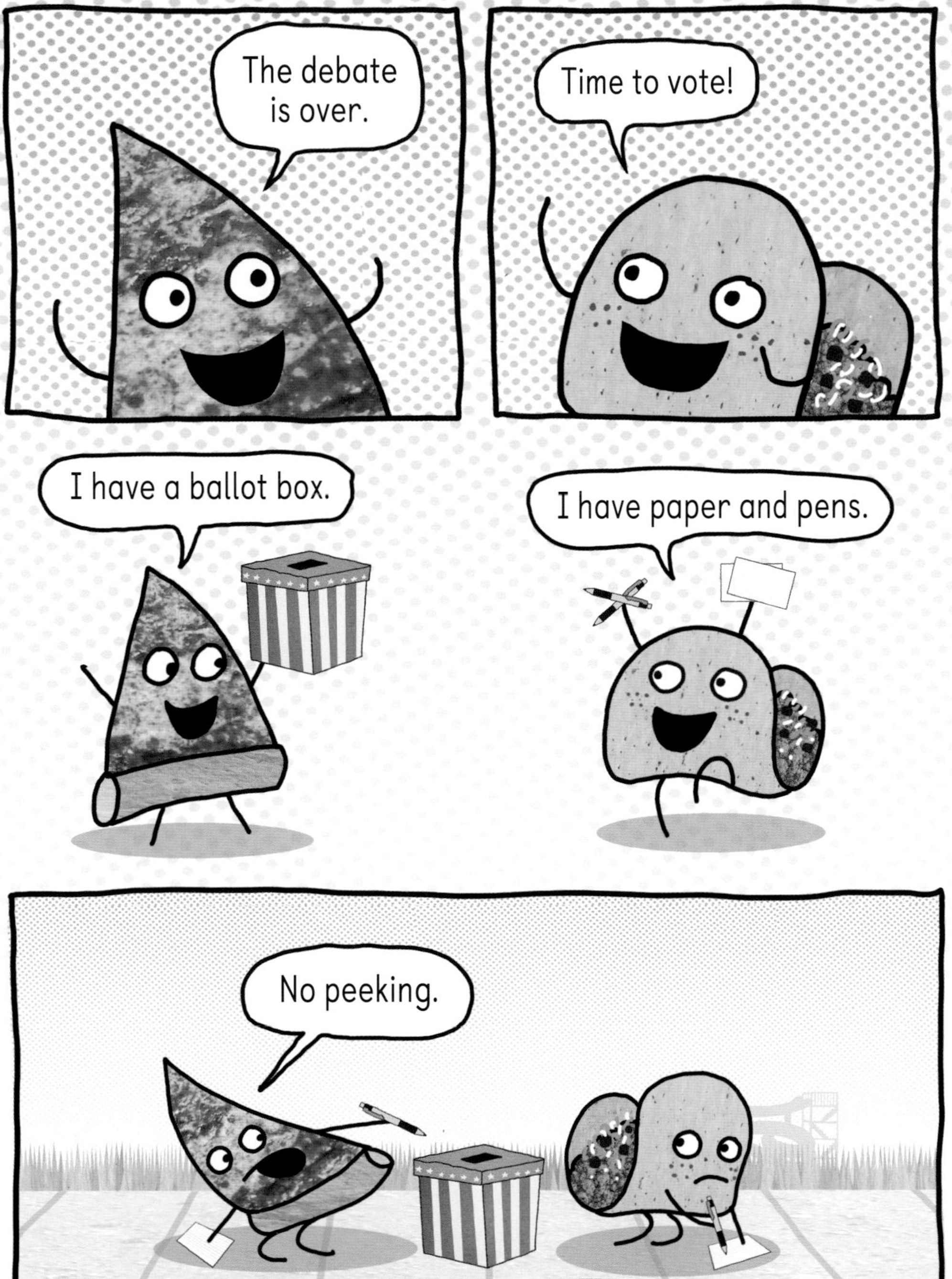
The debate is over.
Time to vote!
I have a ballot box.
I have paper and pens.
No peeking.

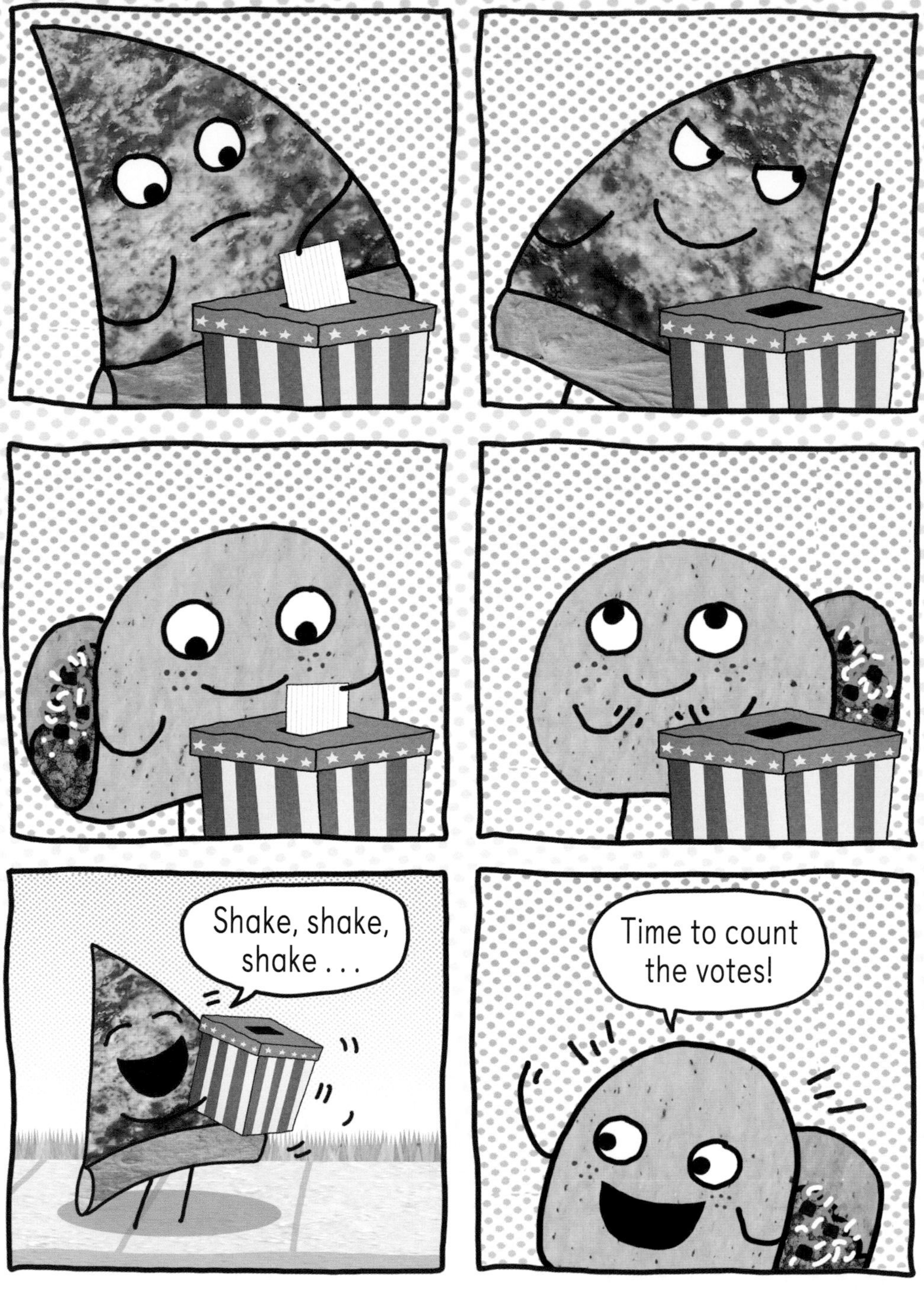
Shake, shake, shake . . .
Time to count the votes!

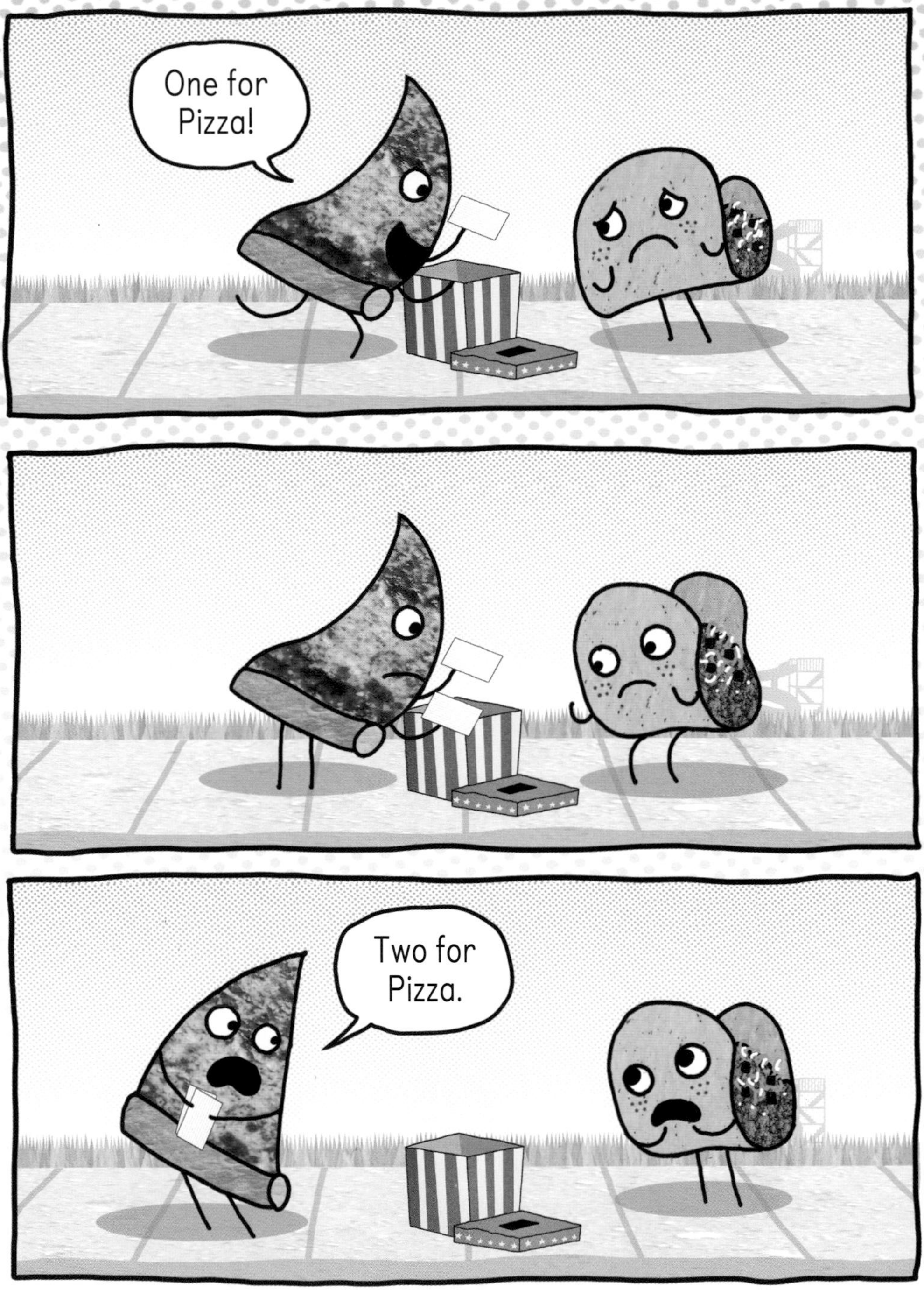
One for Pizza!
Two for Pizza.

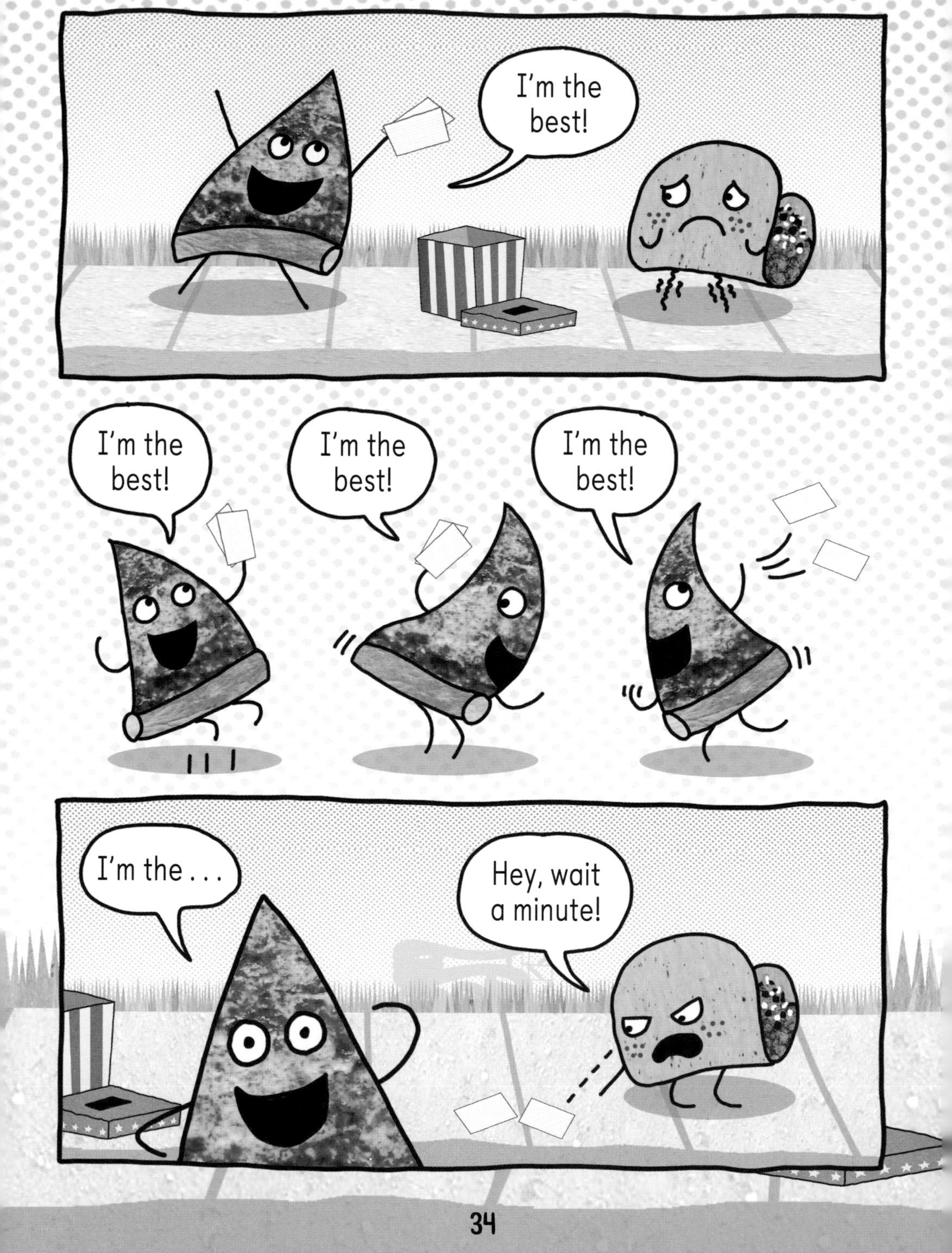
I'm the best!
I'm the best!
I'm the best!
I'm the best!
I'm the . . .
Hey, wait a minute!

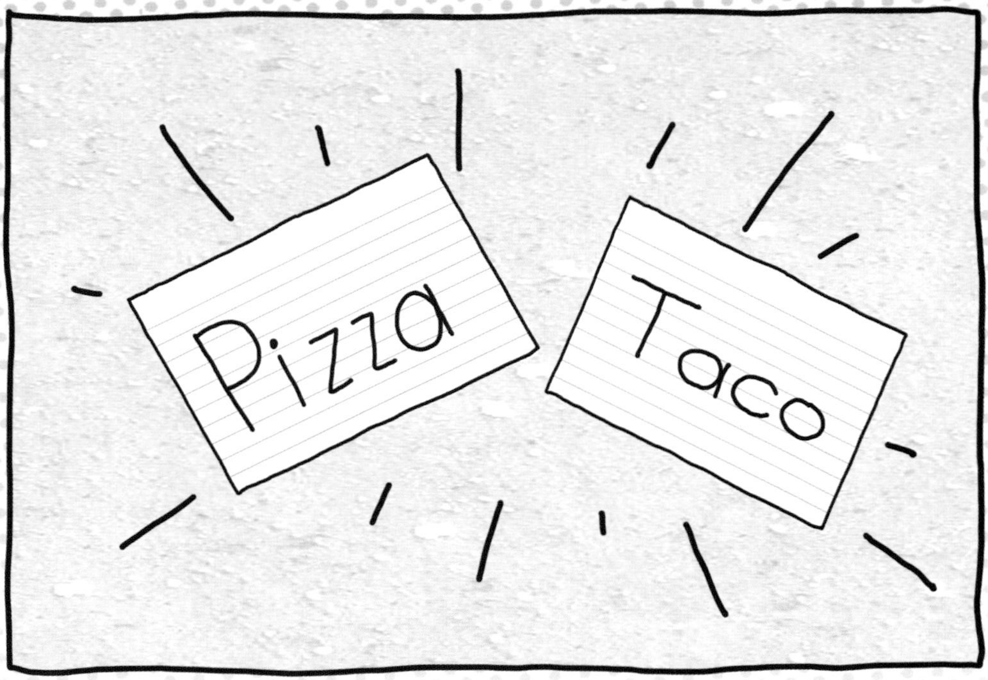
Pizza
Taco

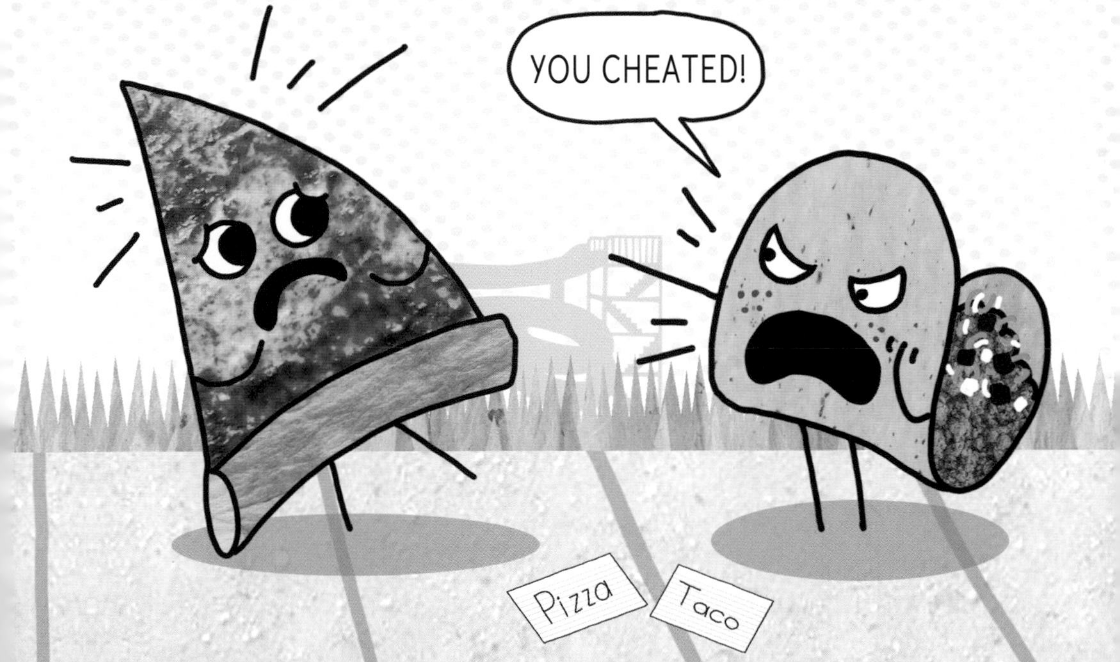
YOU CHEATED!
Pizza
Taco

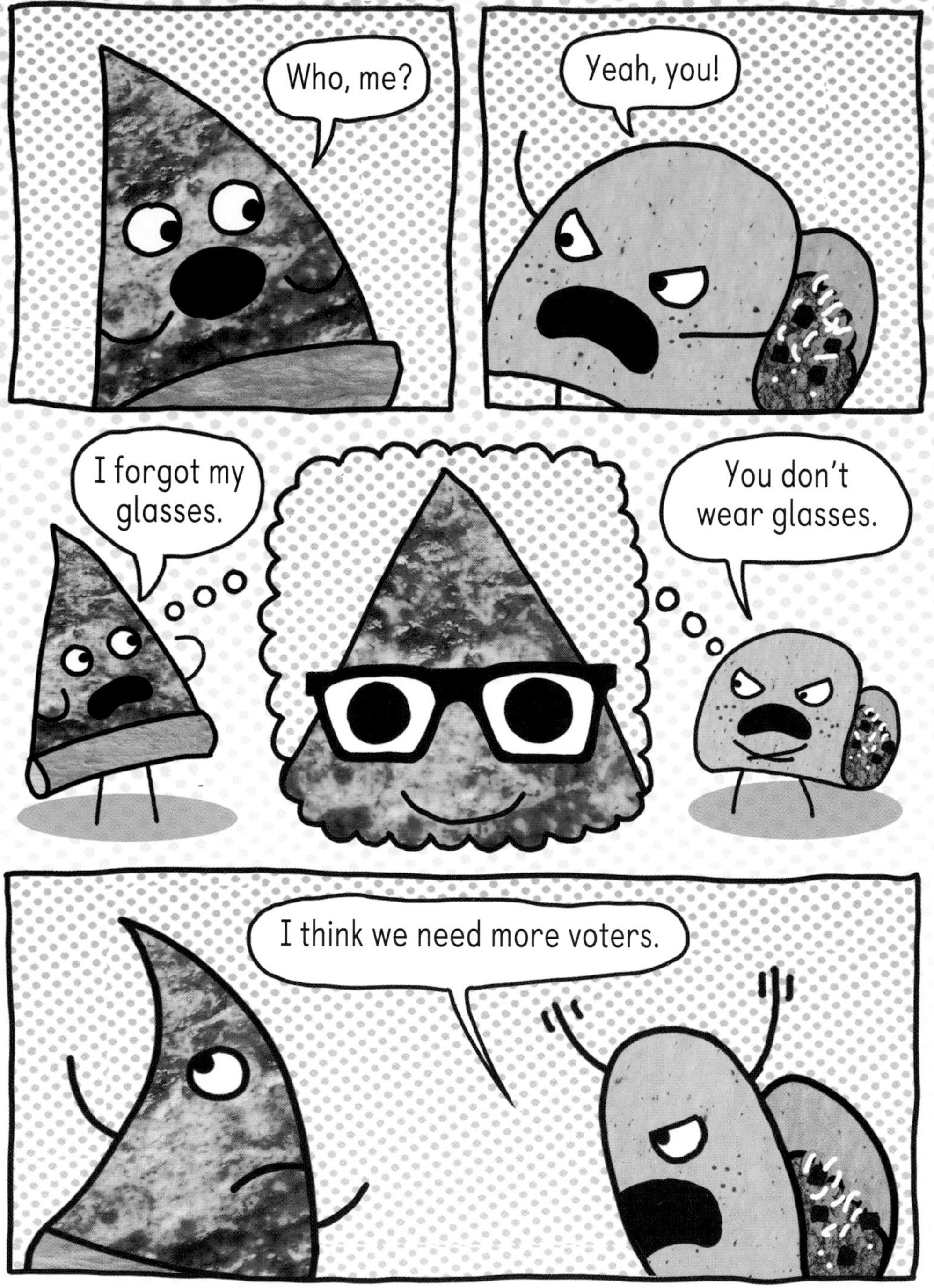
Who, me?
Yeah, you!
I forgot my glasses.
You don't wear glasses.
I think we need more voters.

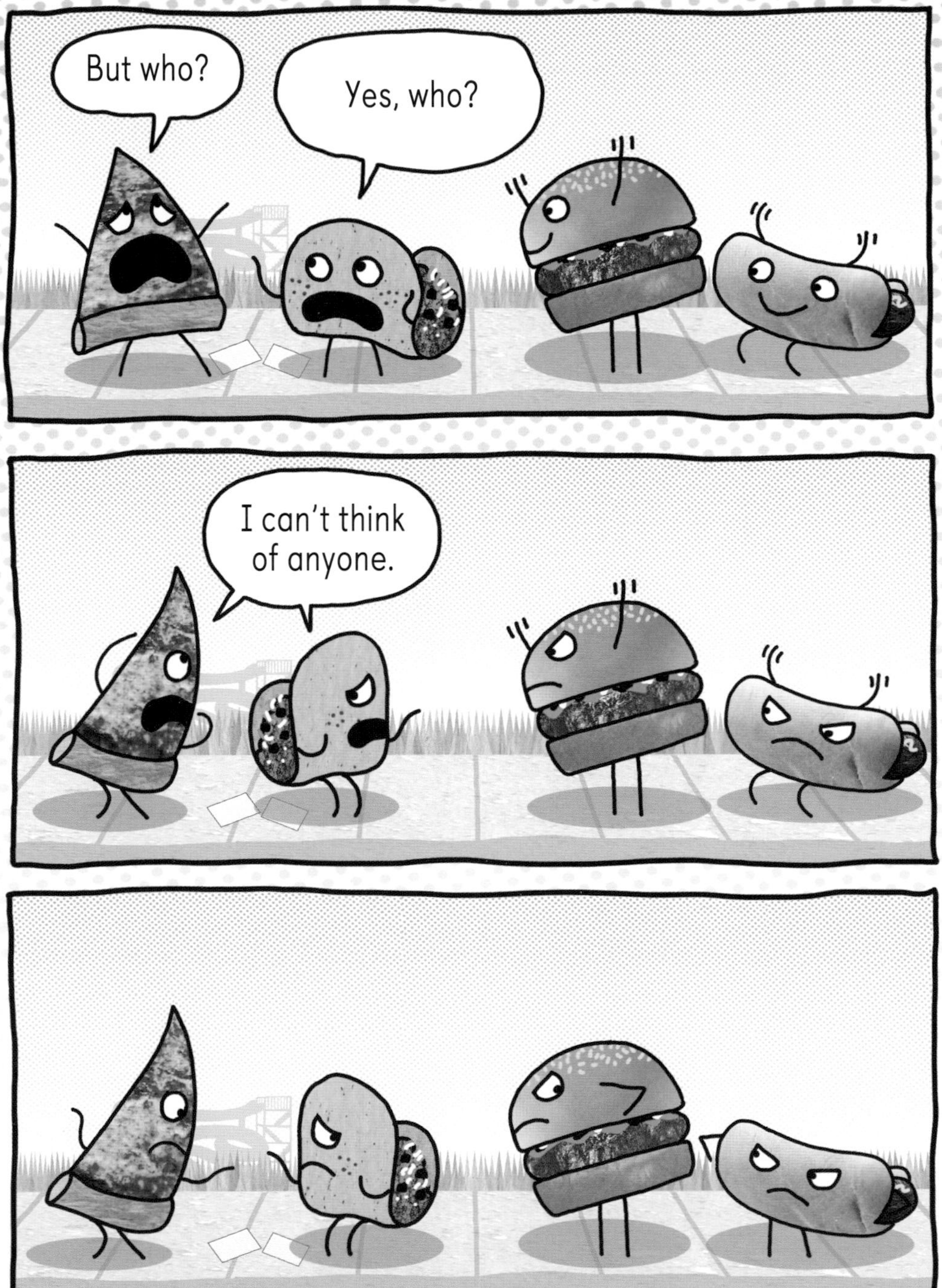
But who?
Yes, who?
I can't think of anyone.

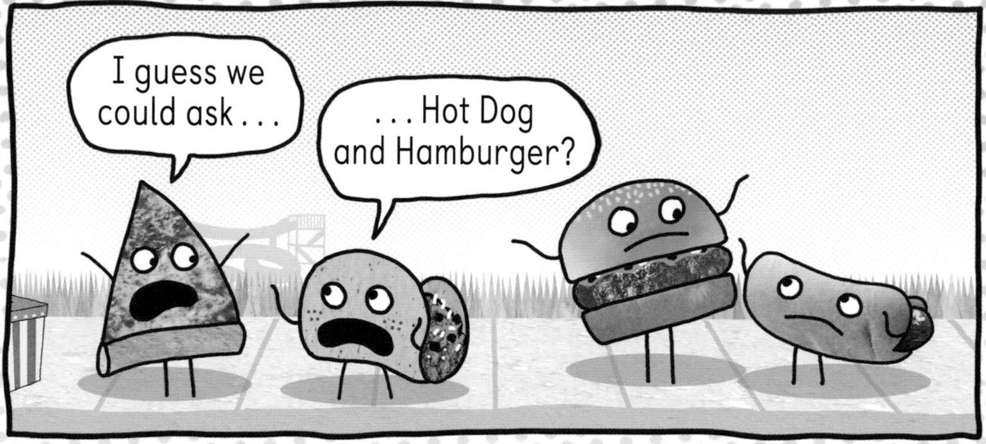
I guess we could ask . . .
. . . Hot Dog and Hamburger?

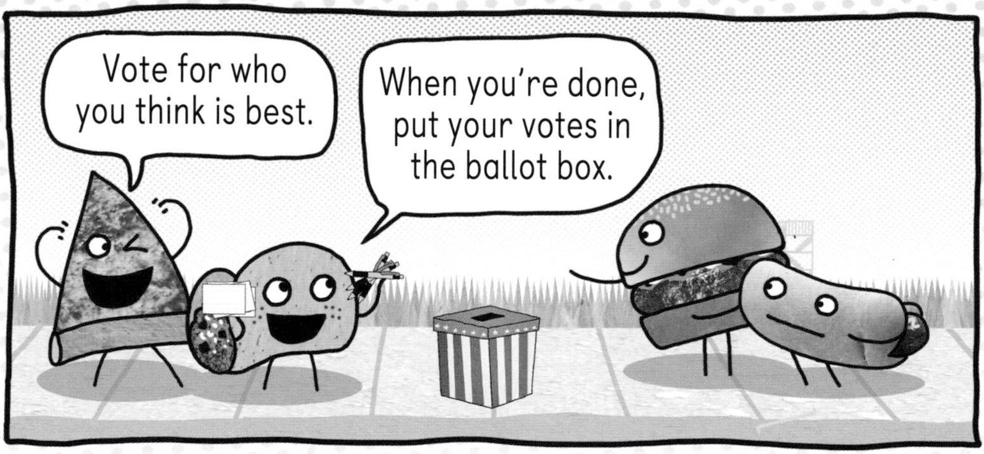
Vote for who you think is best.
When you're done, put your votes in the ballot box.

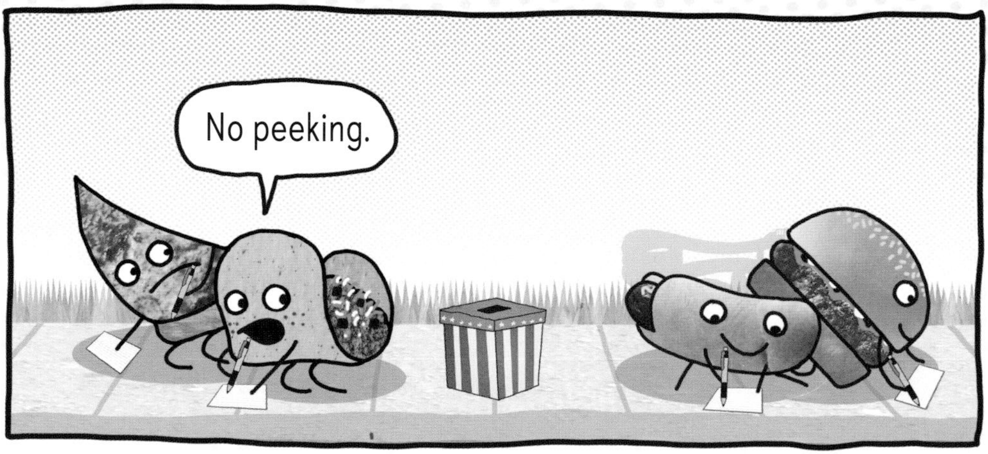
No peeking.

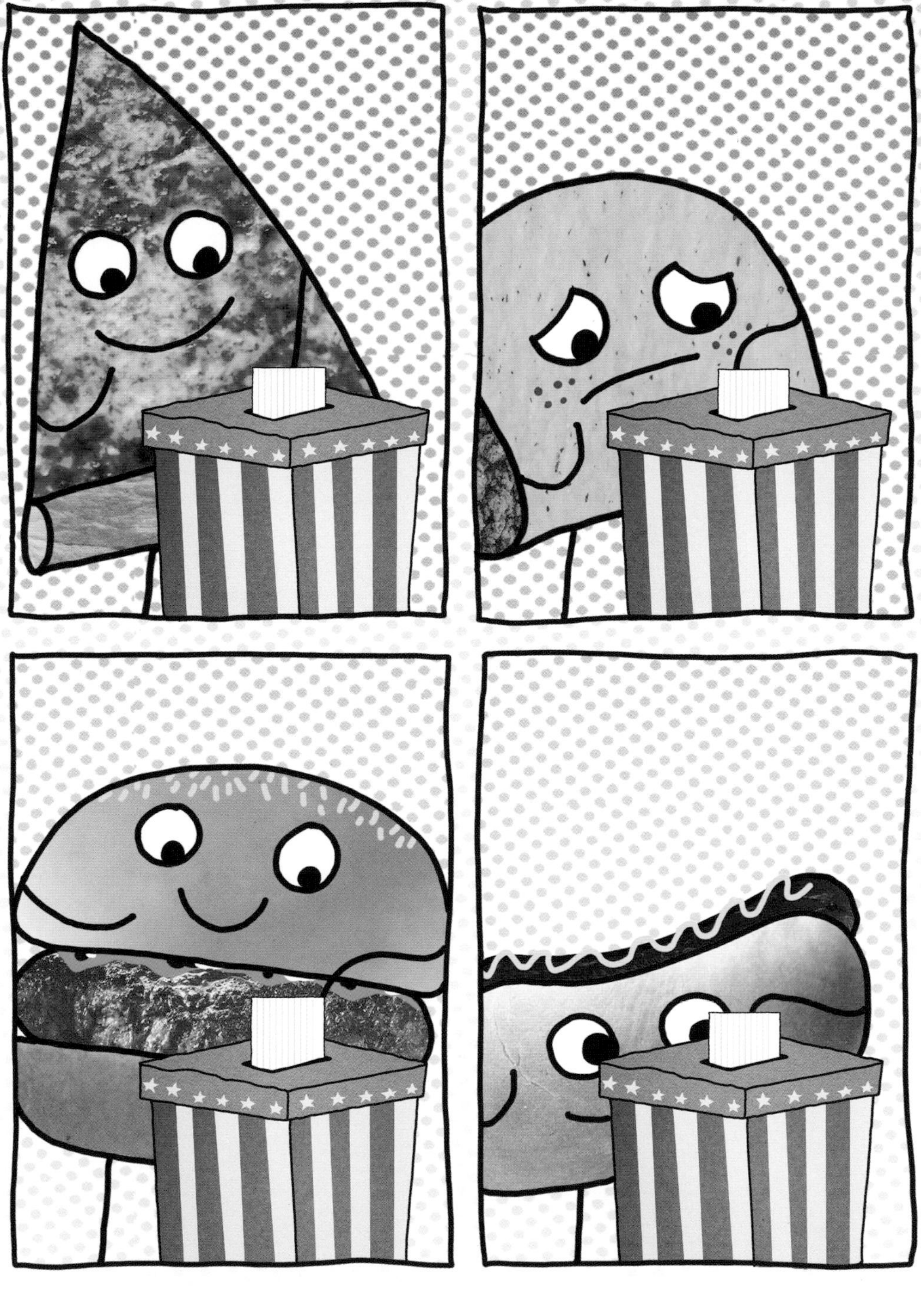

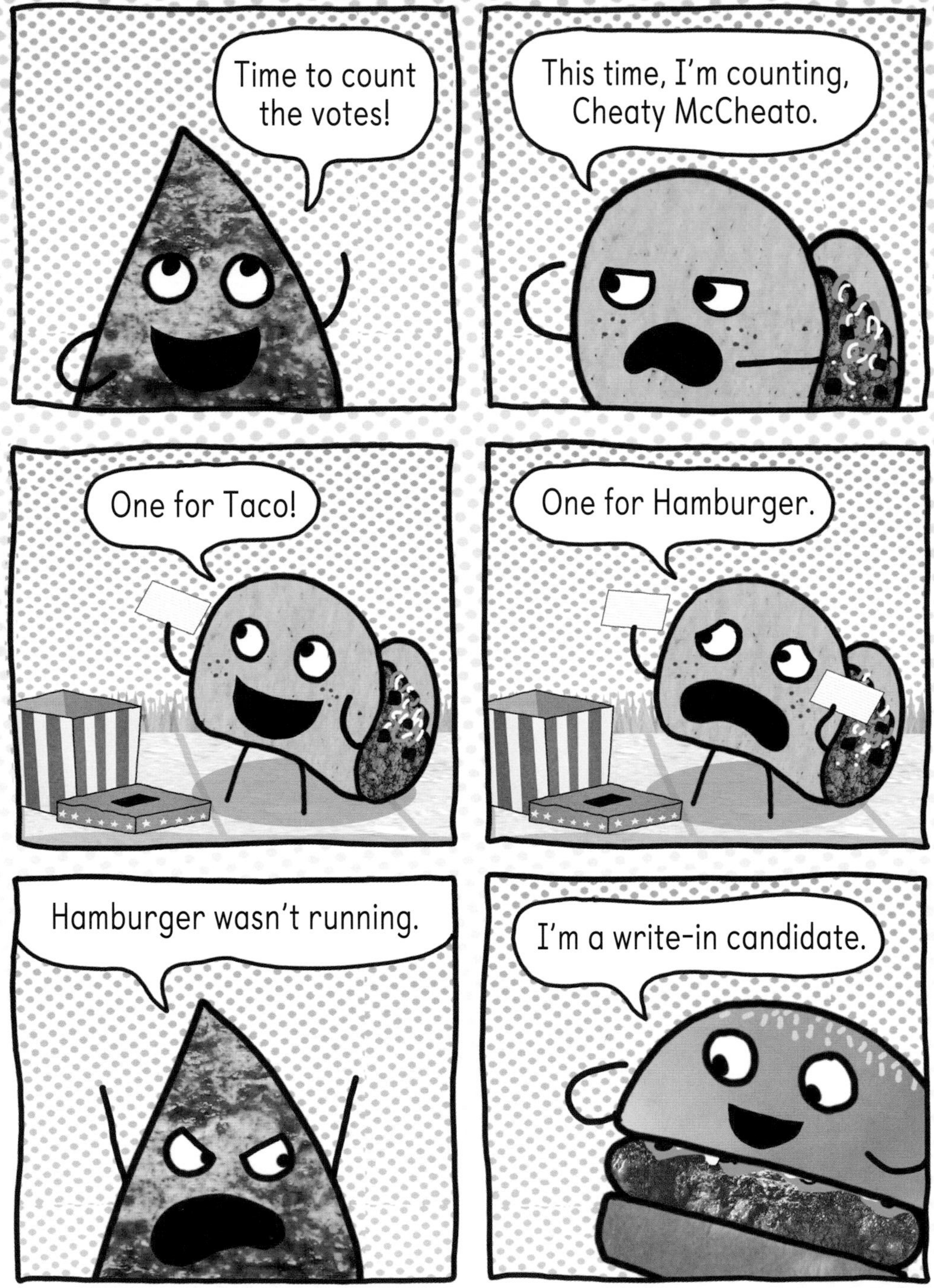
Time to count the votes!
This time, I'm counting, Cheaty McCheato.
One for Taco!
One for Hamburger.
Hamburger wasn't running.
I'm a write-in candidate.

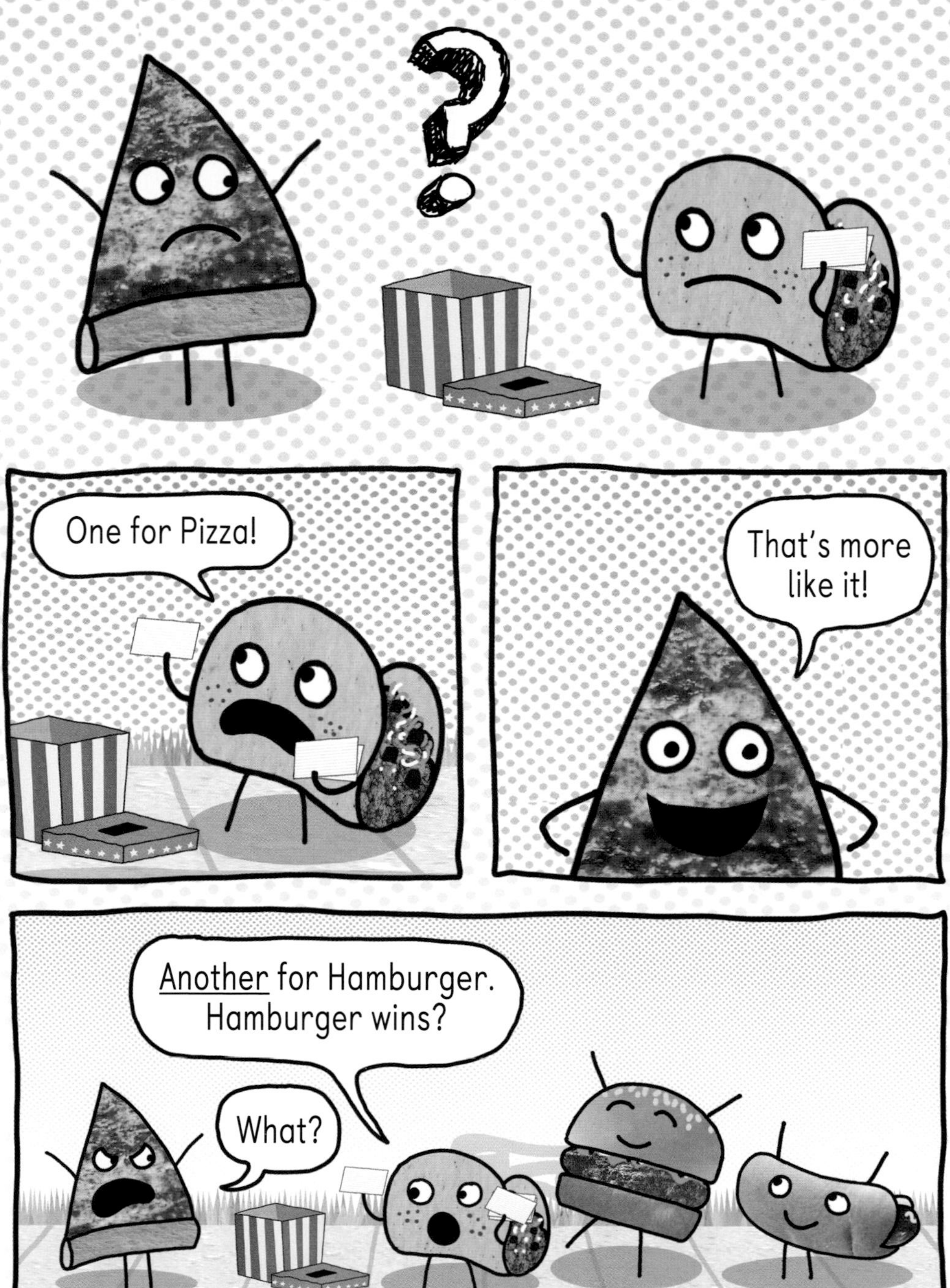
One for Pizza!
That's more like it!
Another for Hamburger. Hamburger wins?
What?

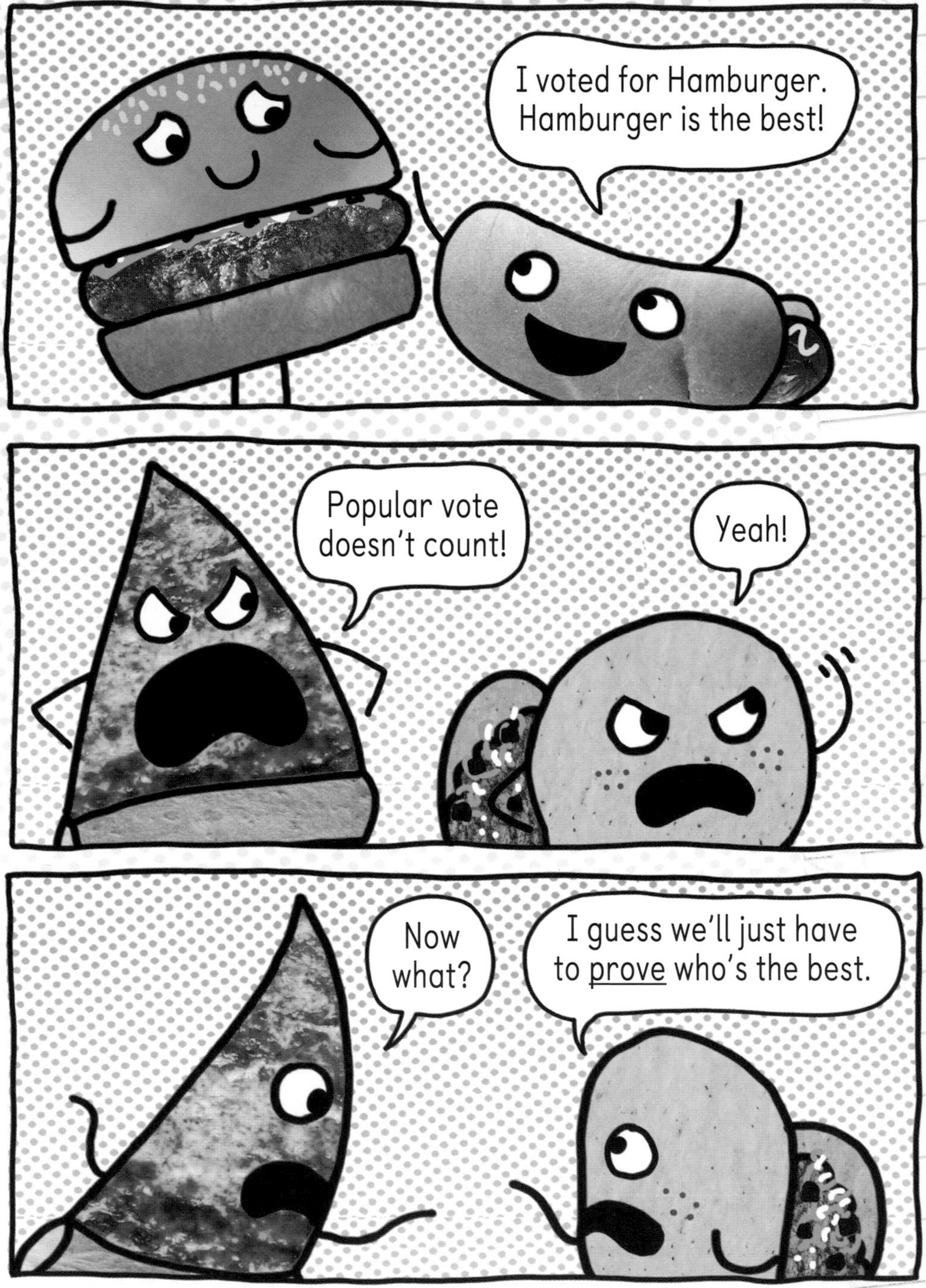
I voted for Hamburger. Hamburger is the best!
Popular vote doesn't count!
Yeah!
Now what?
I guess we'll just have to prove who's the best.

Chapter 4
PIZZA and TACO Prove Who's Best

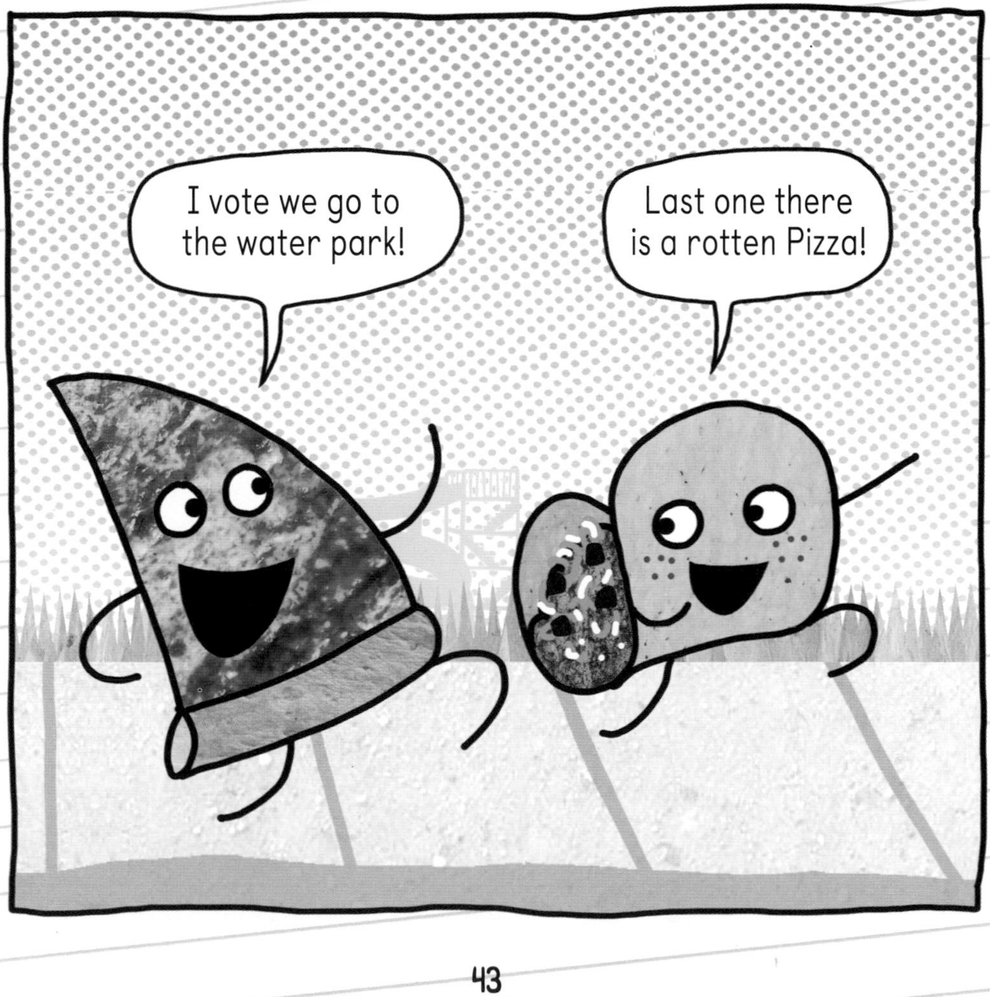

I vote we go to the water park!
Last one there is a rotten Pizza!

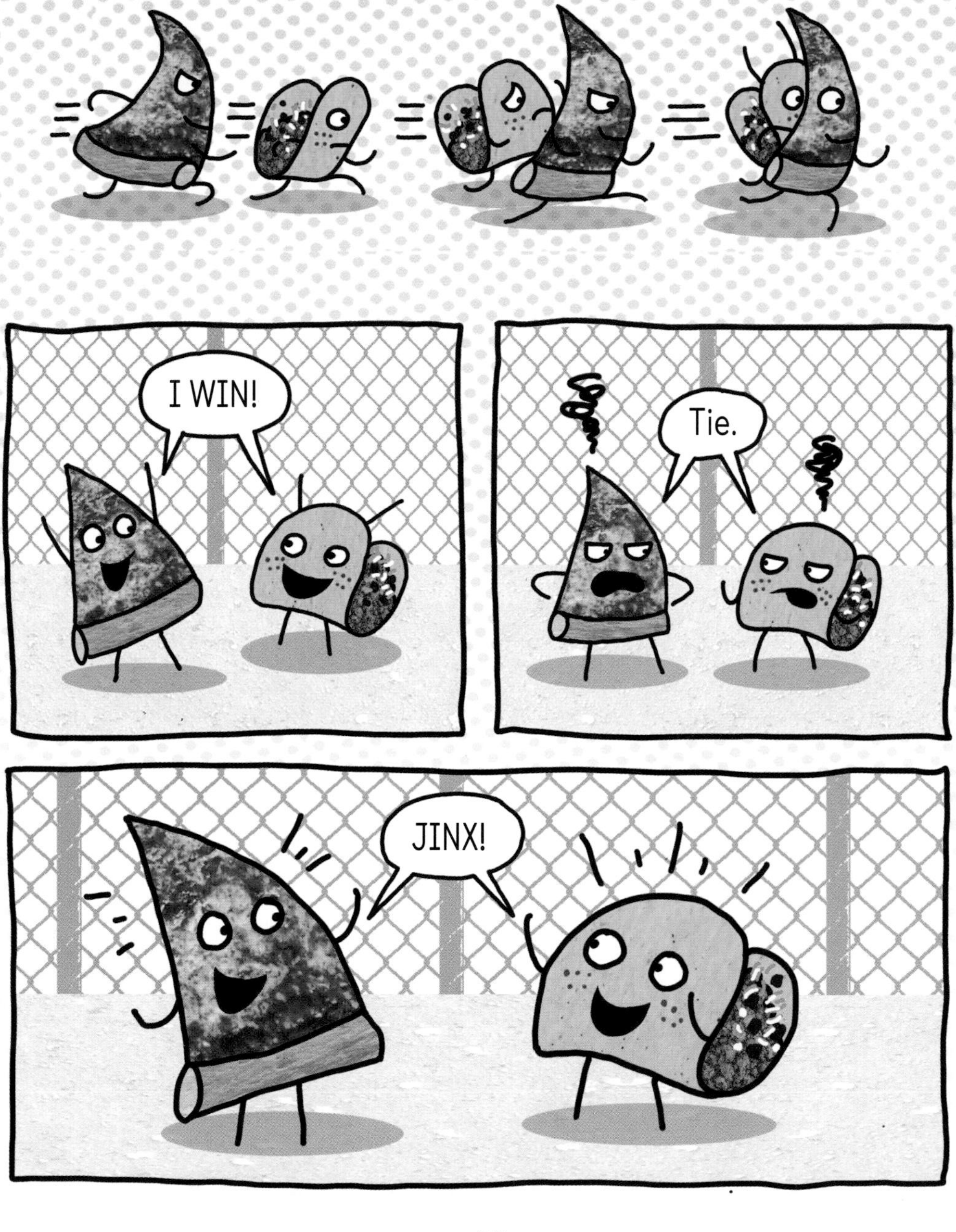
I WIN!
Tie.
JINX!

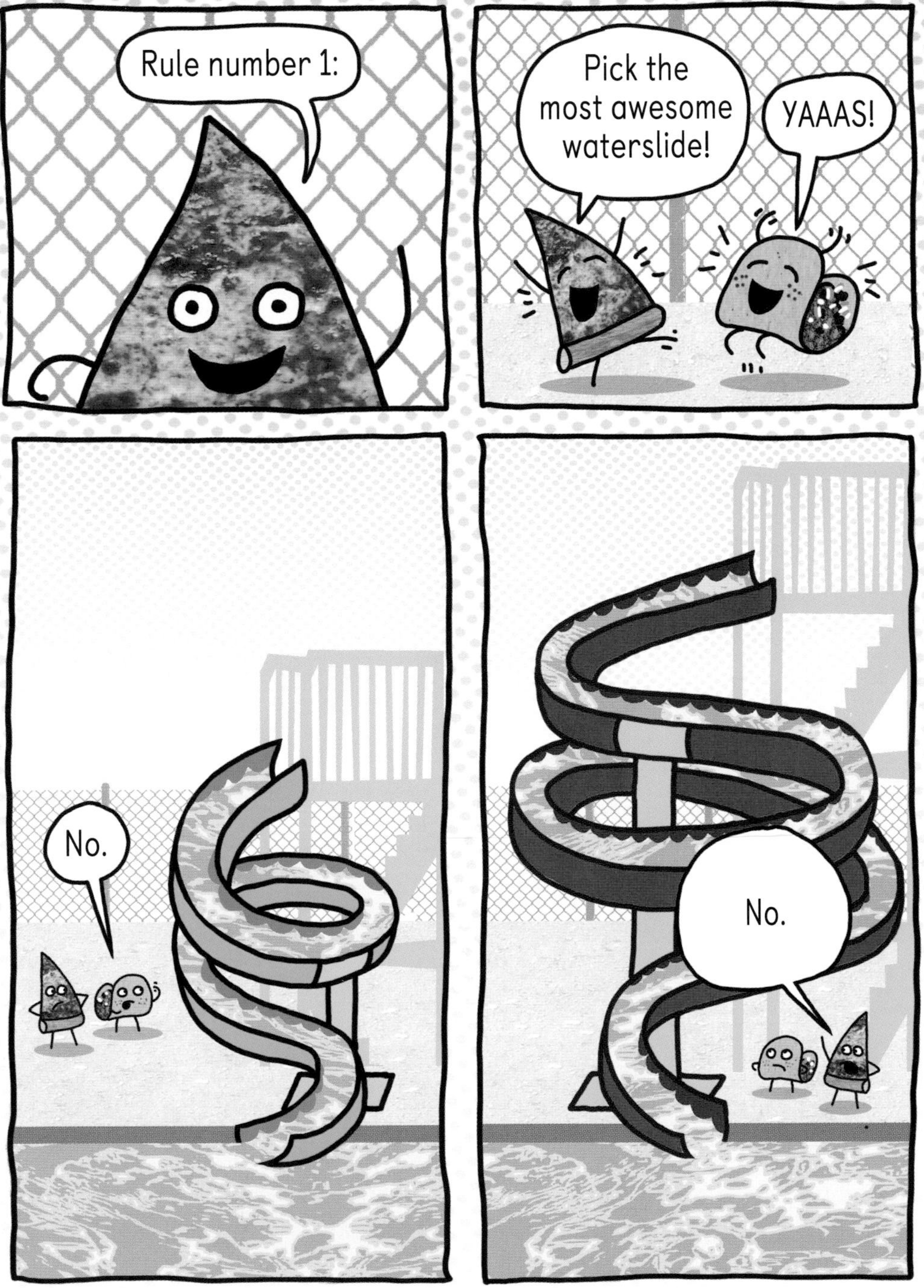
Rule number 1:
Pick the most awesome waterslide!
YAAAS!
No.
No.

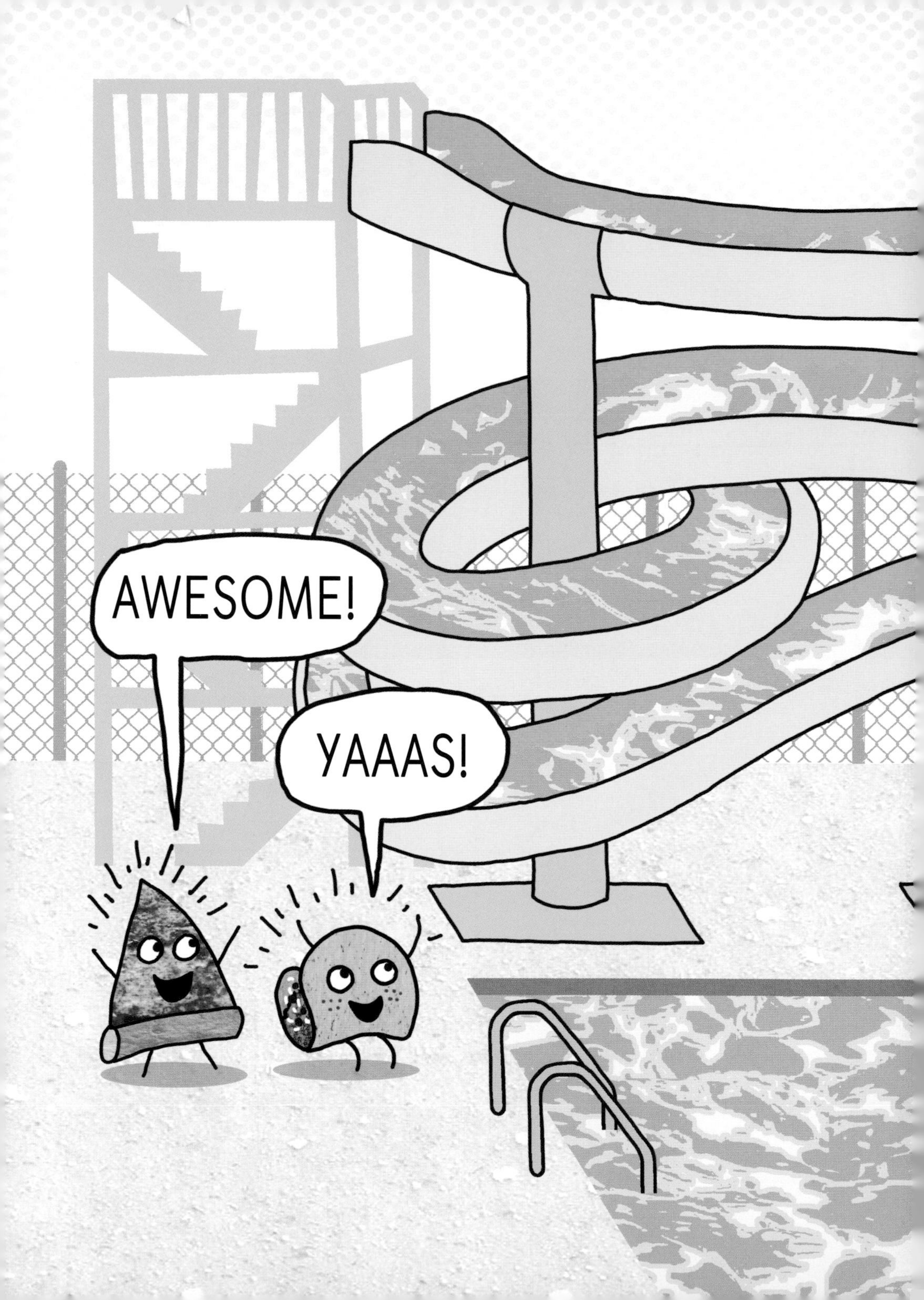
AWESOME!
YAAAS!

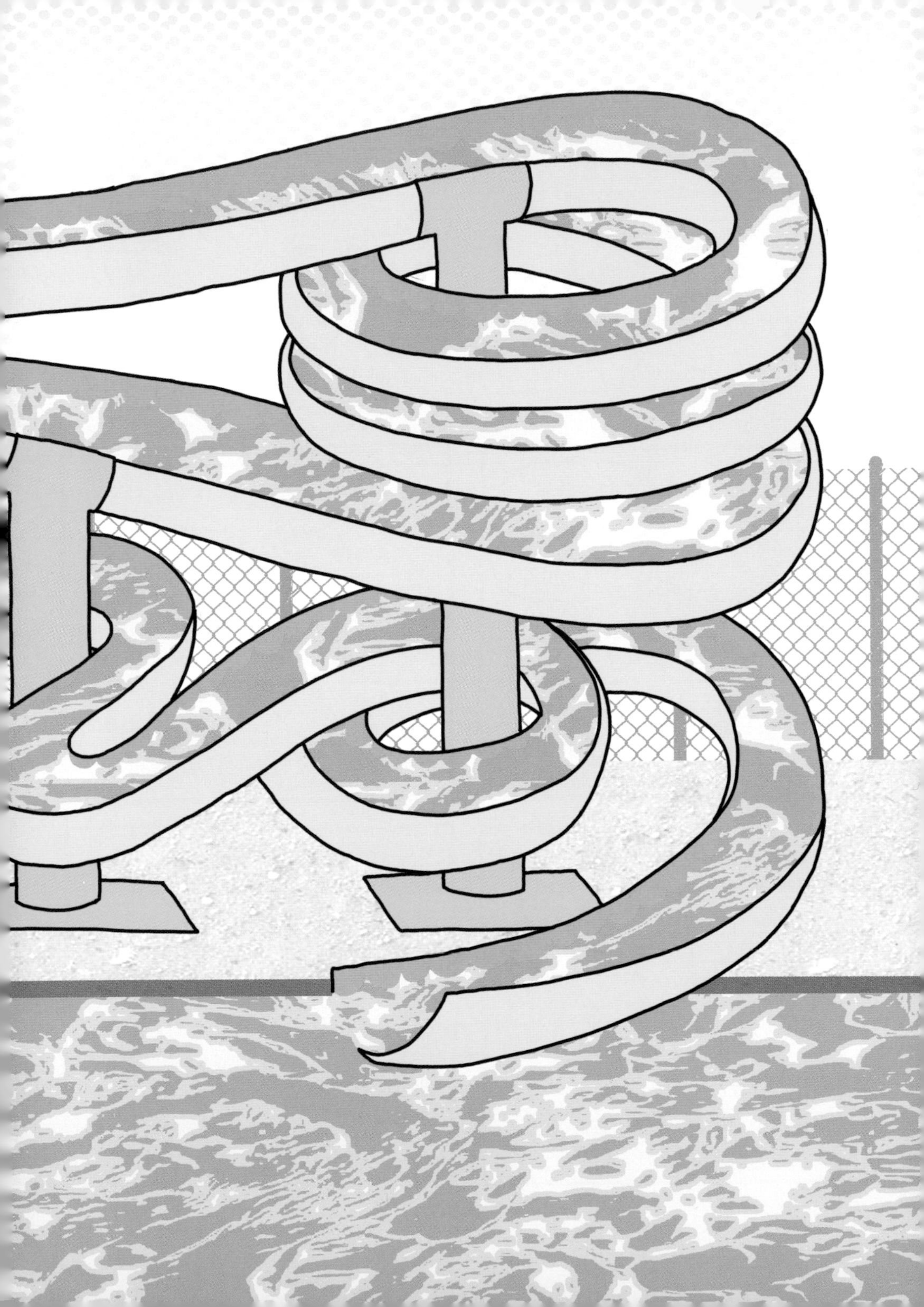

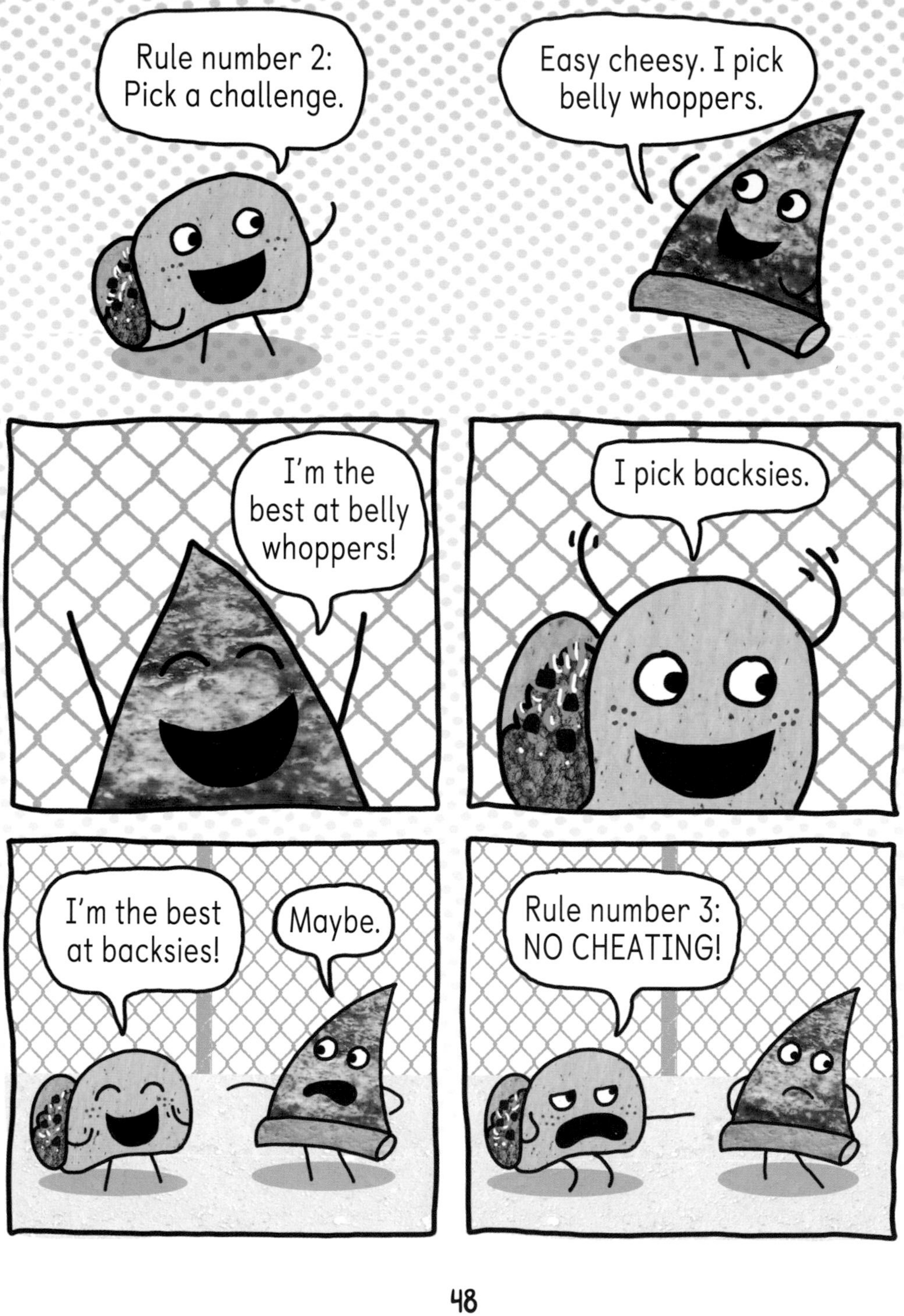
Rule number 2:
Pick a challenge.
Easy cheesy. I pick
belly whoppers.
I'm the
best at belly
whoppers!
I pick backsies.
I'm the best
at backsies!
Maybe.
Rule number 3:
NO CHEATING!

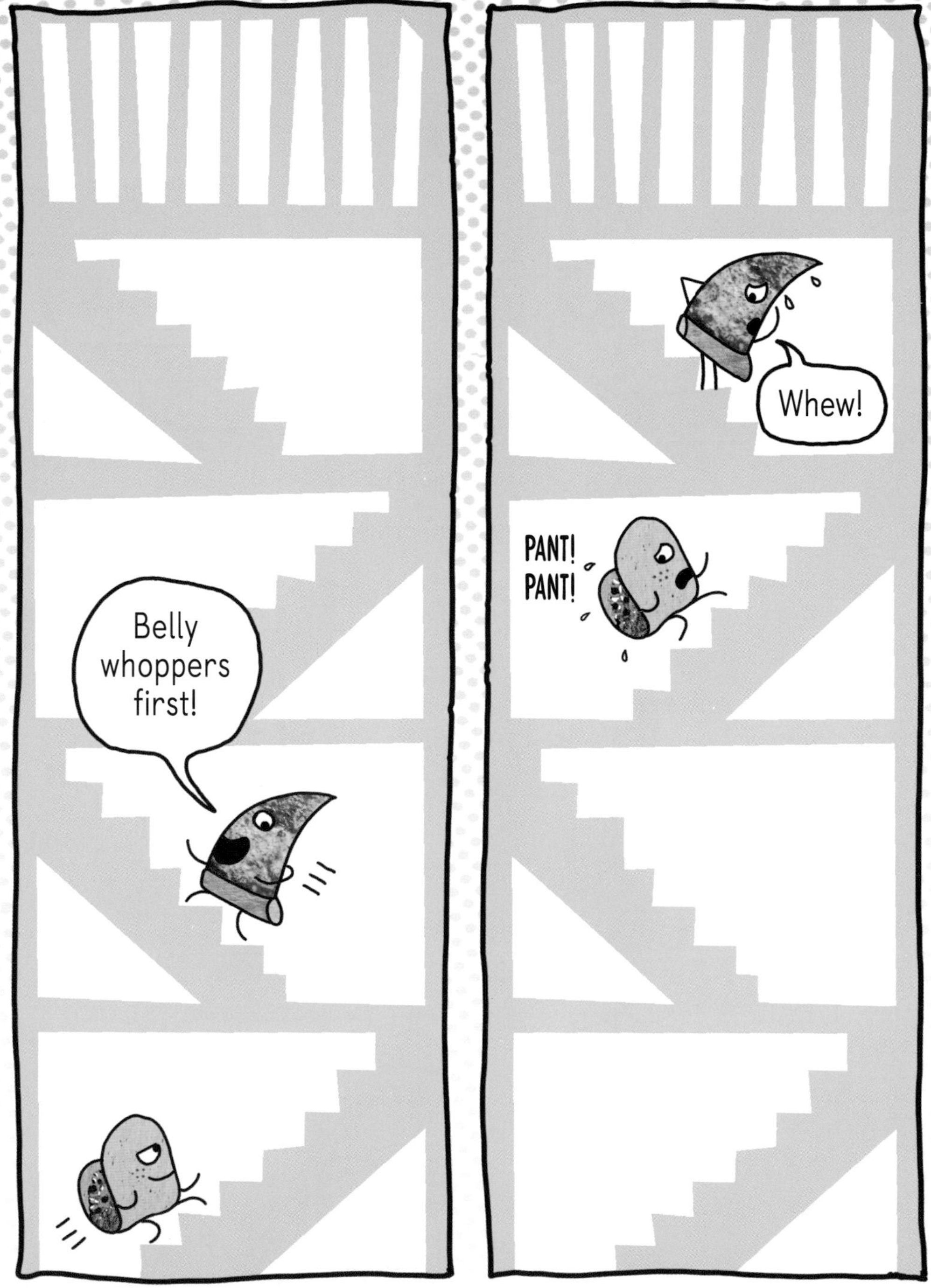
Belly whoppers first!
Whew!
PANT!
PANT!

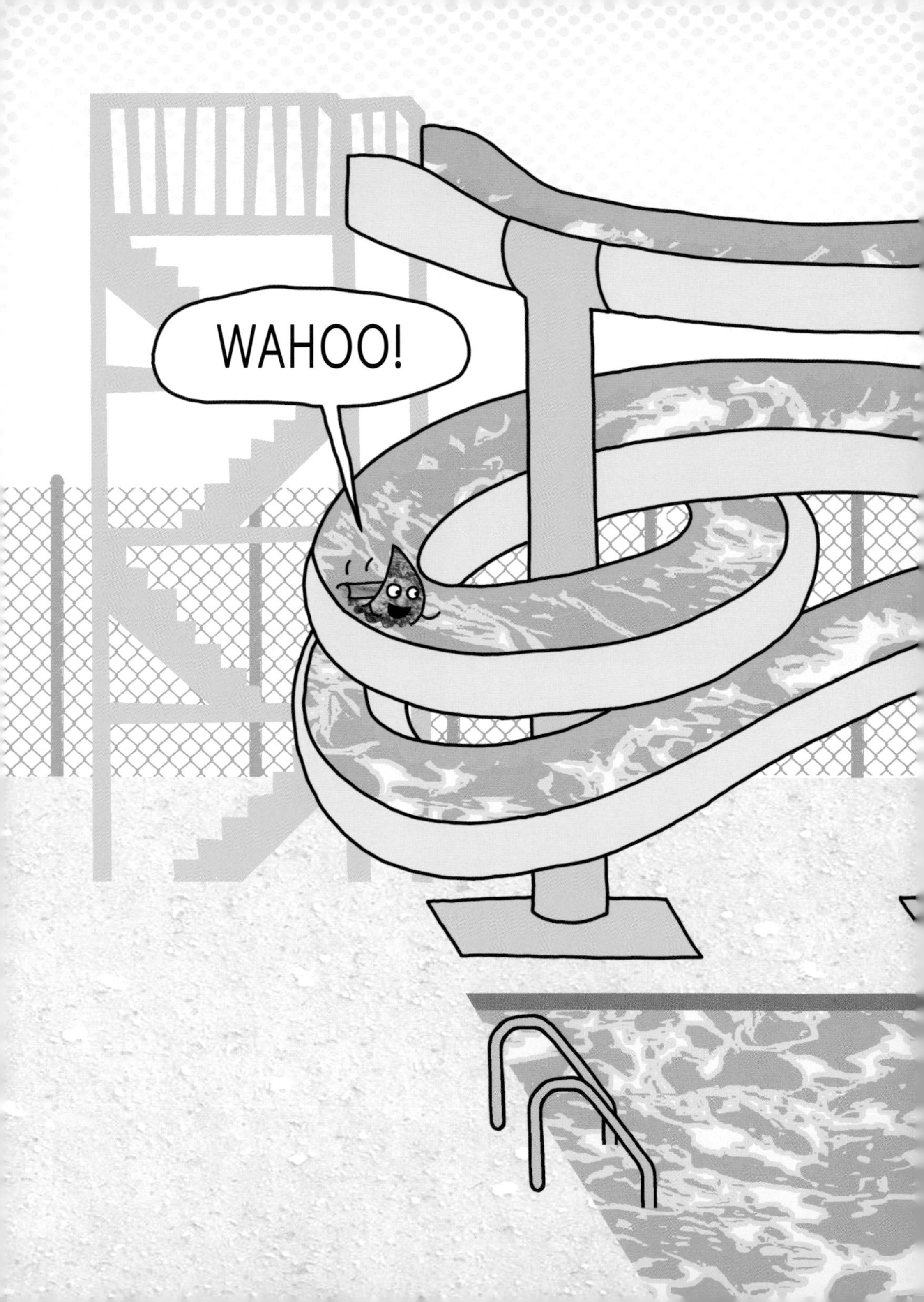
WAHOO!

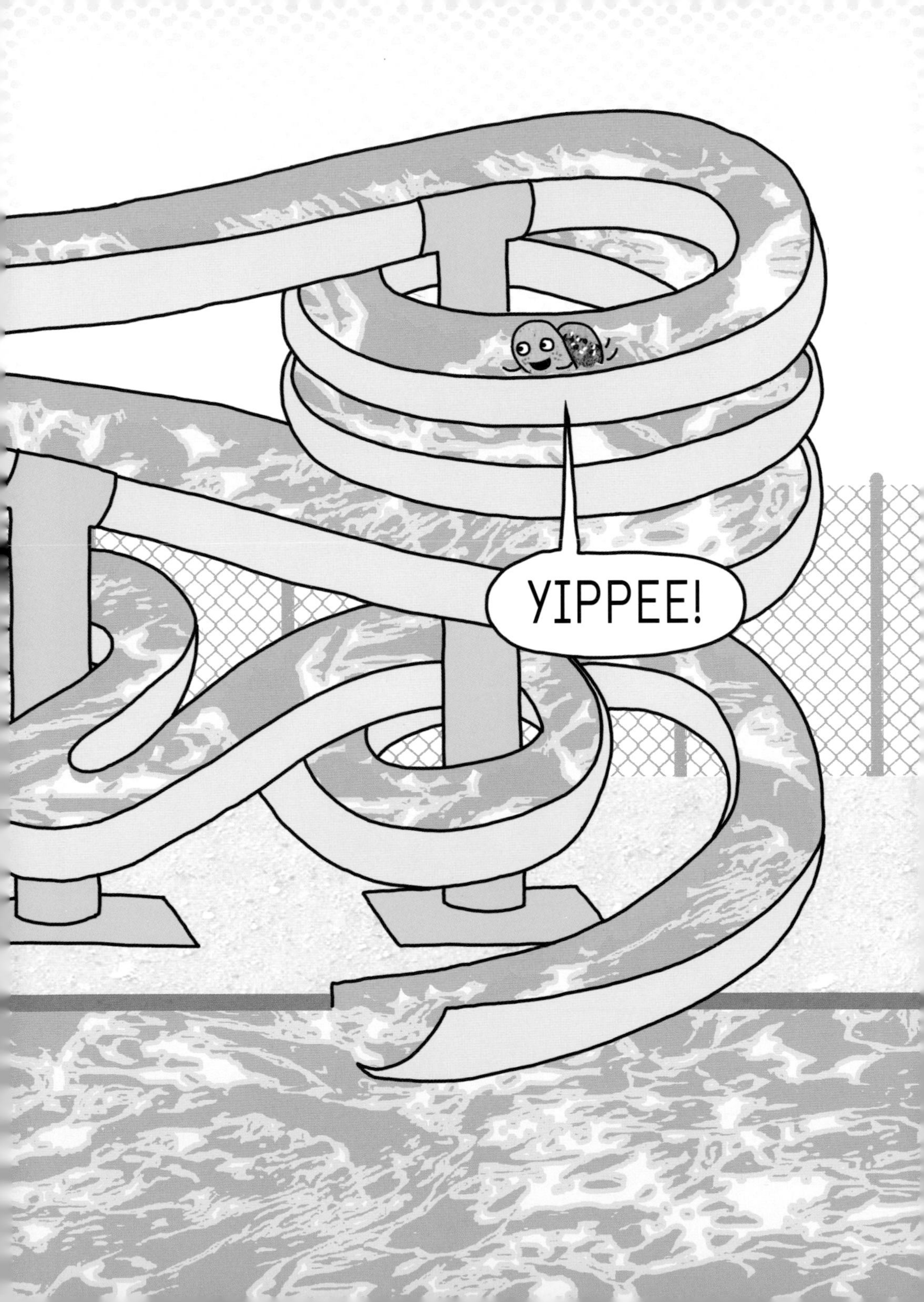
YIPPEE!

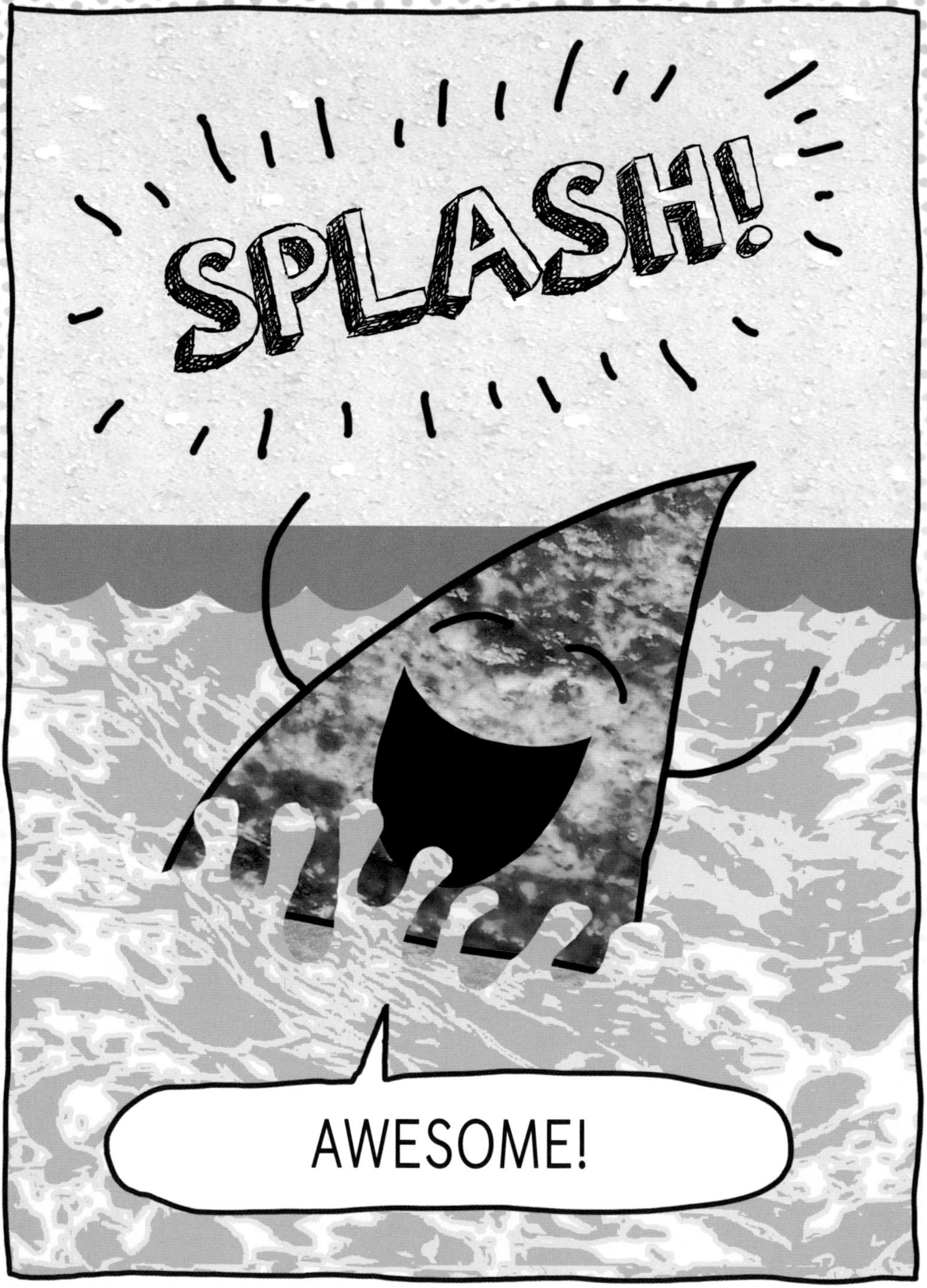
SPLASH!
AWESOME!

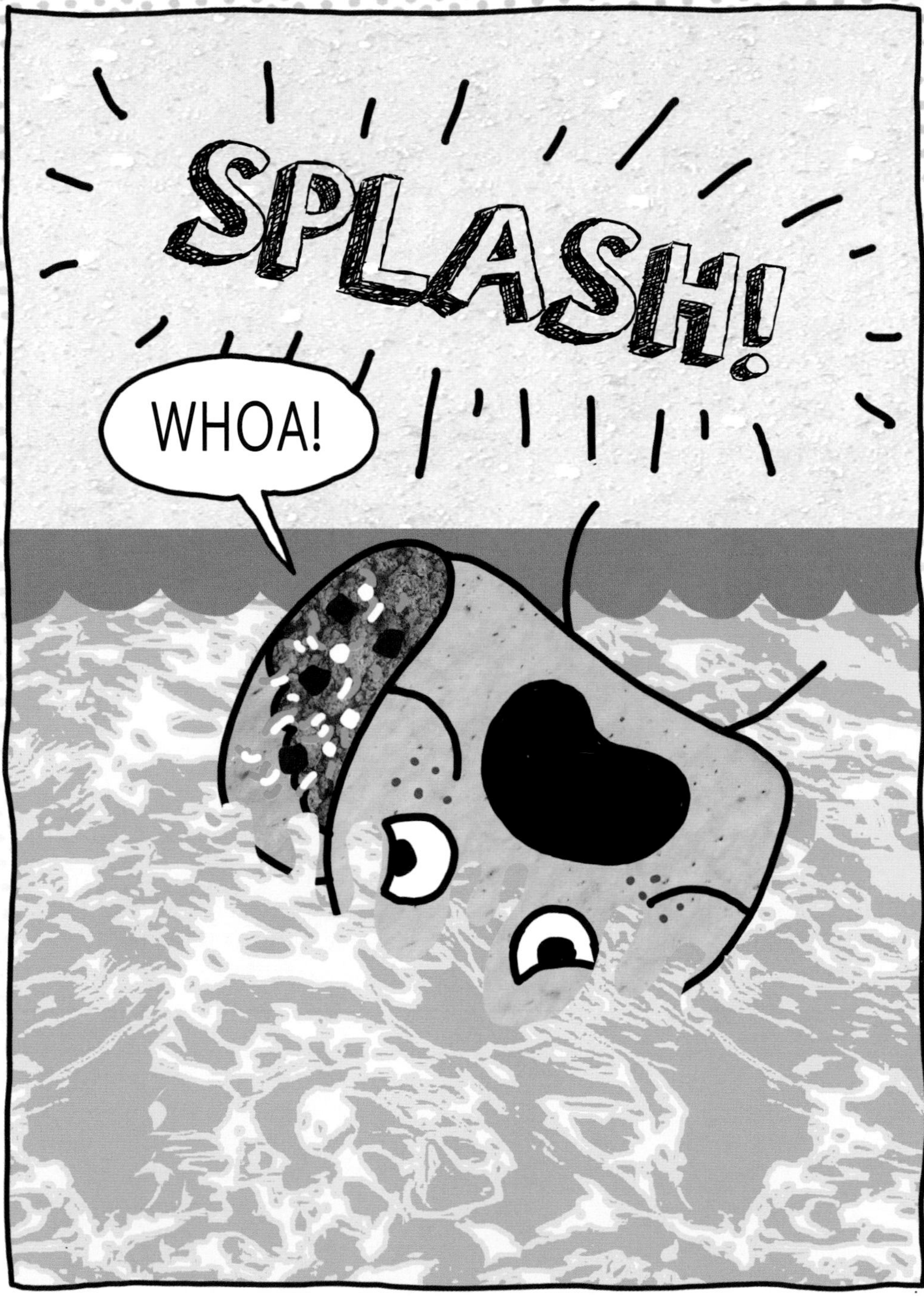
SPLASH!
WHOA!

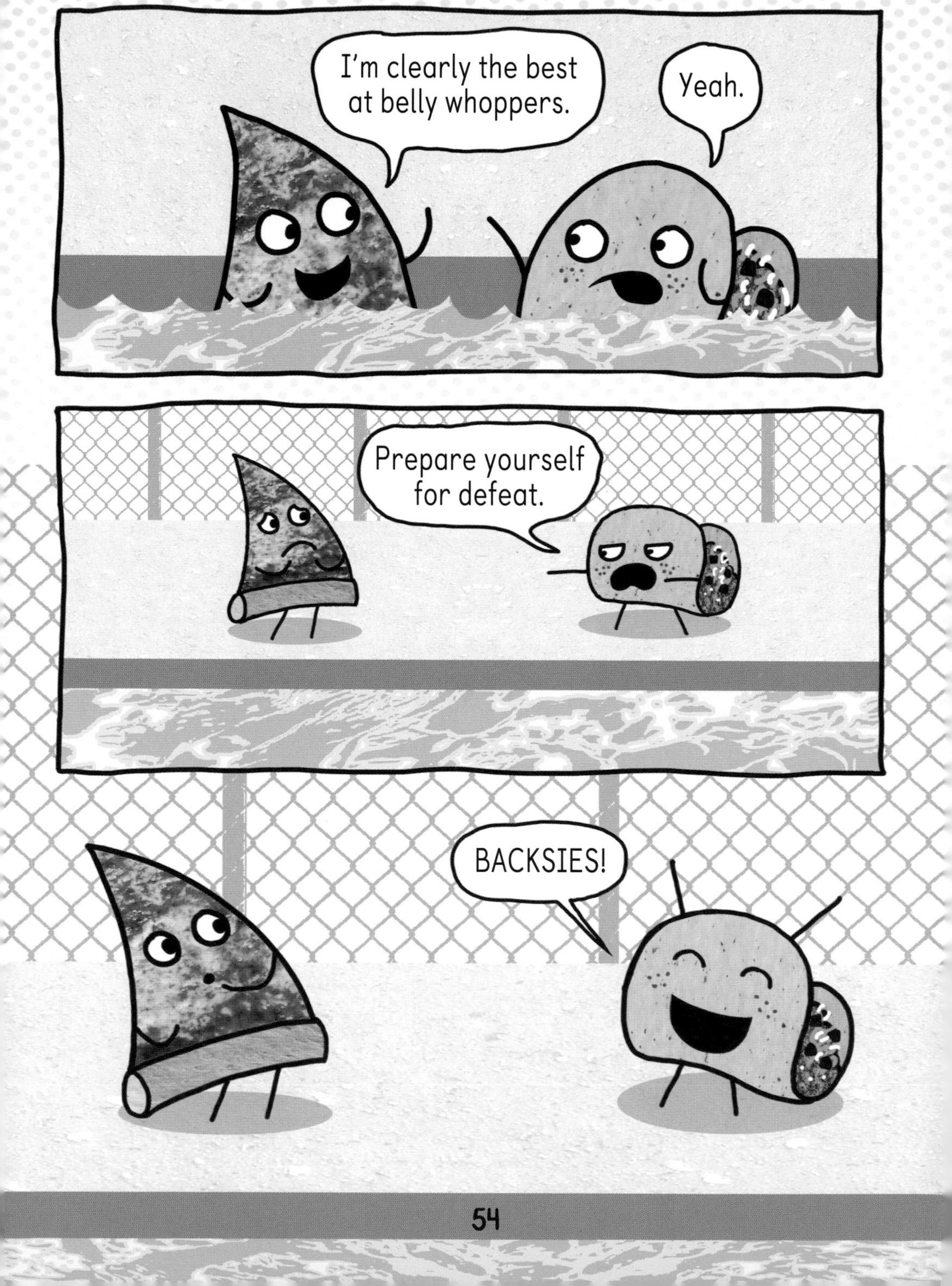
I'm clearly the best at belly whoppers.
Yeah.
Prepare yourself for defeat.
BACKSIES!

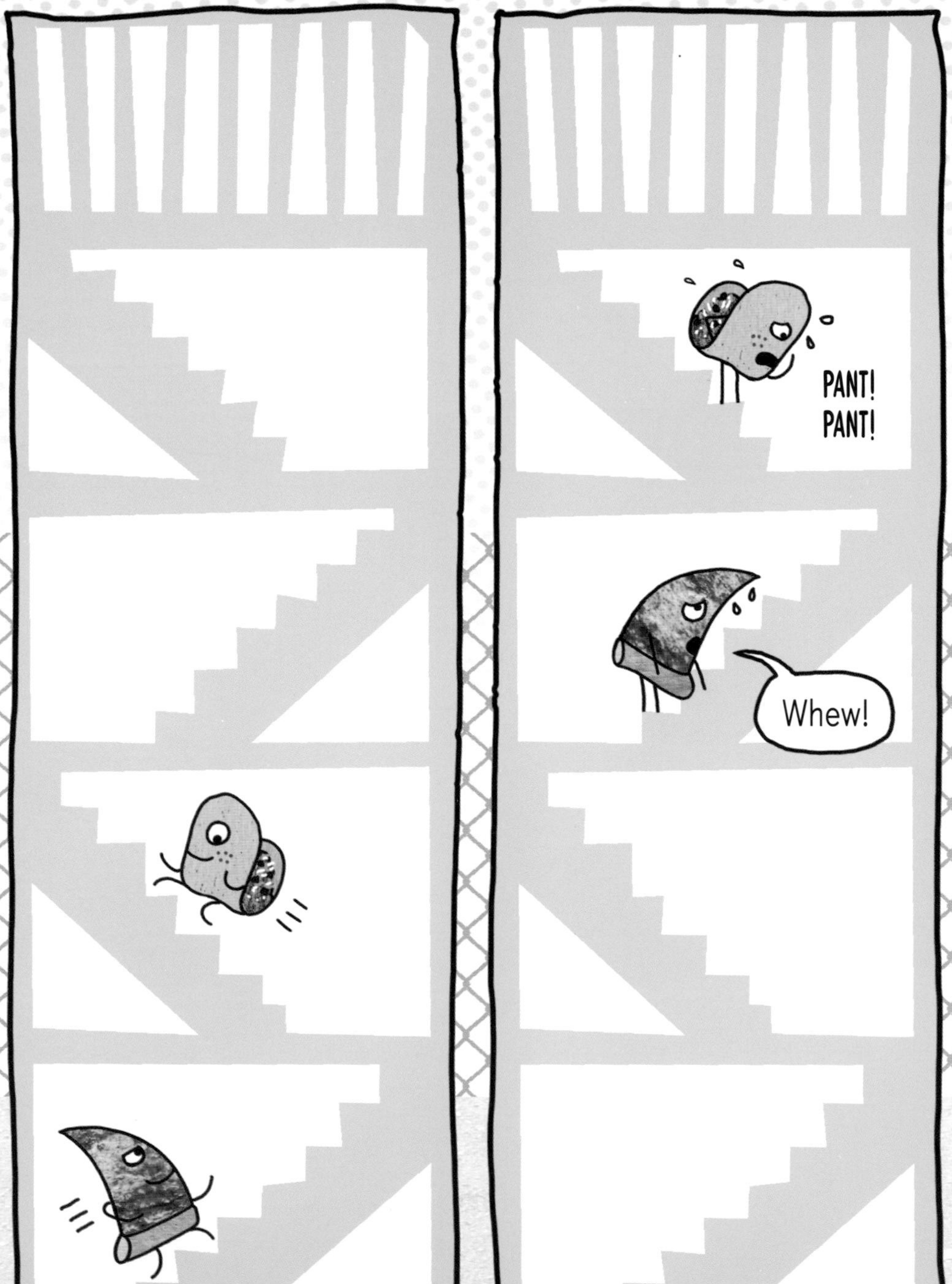
PANT!
PANT!
Whew!

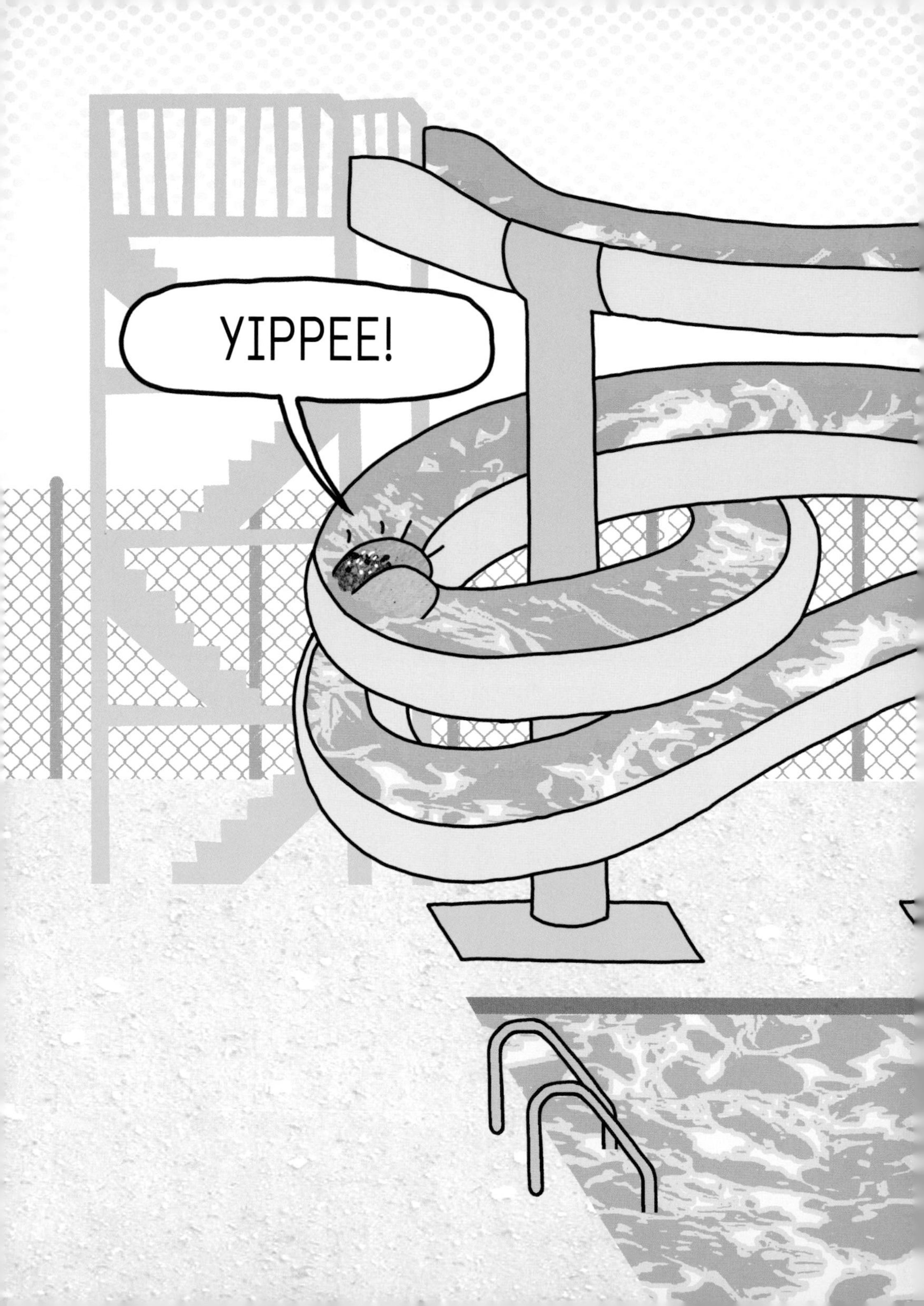
YIPPEE!

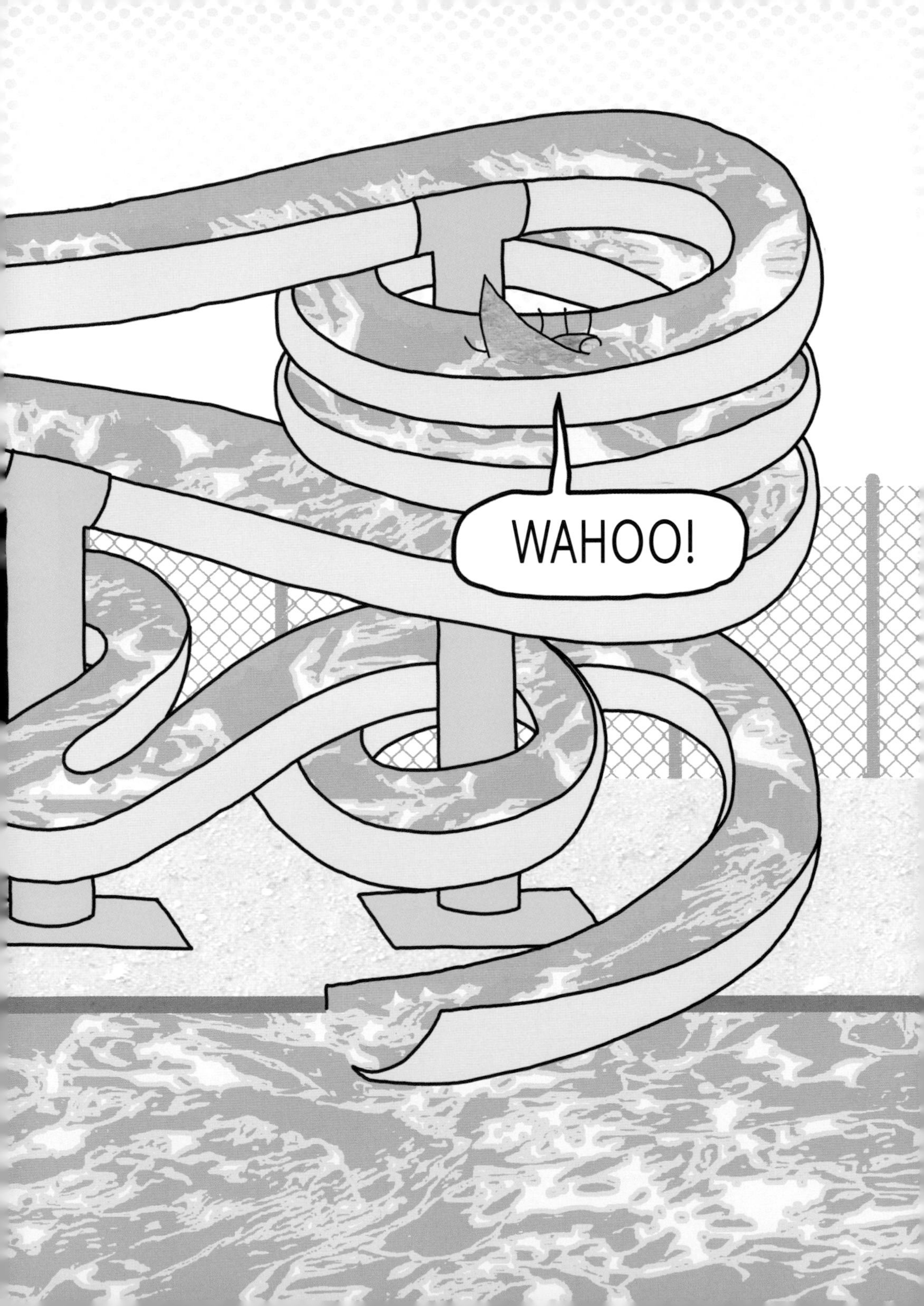
WAHOO!

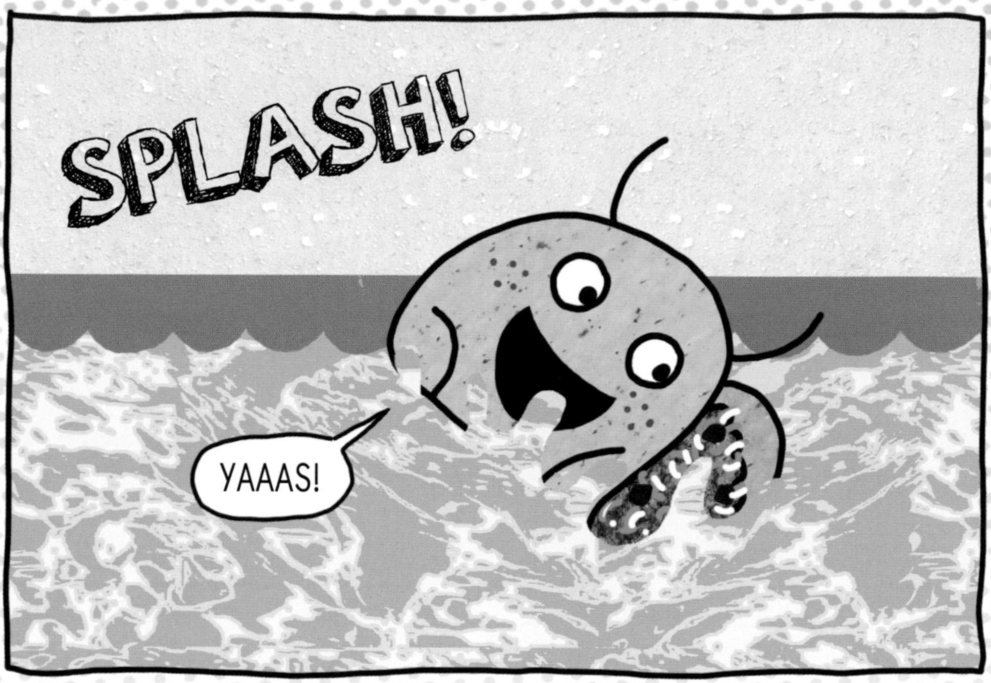
SPLASH!
YAAAS!

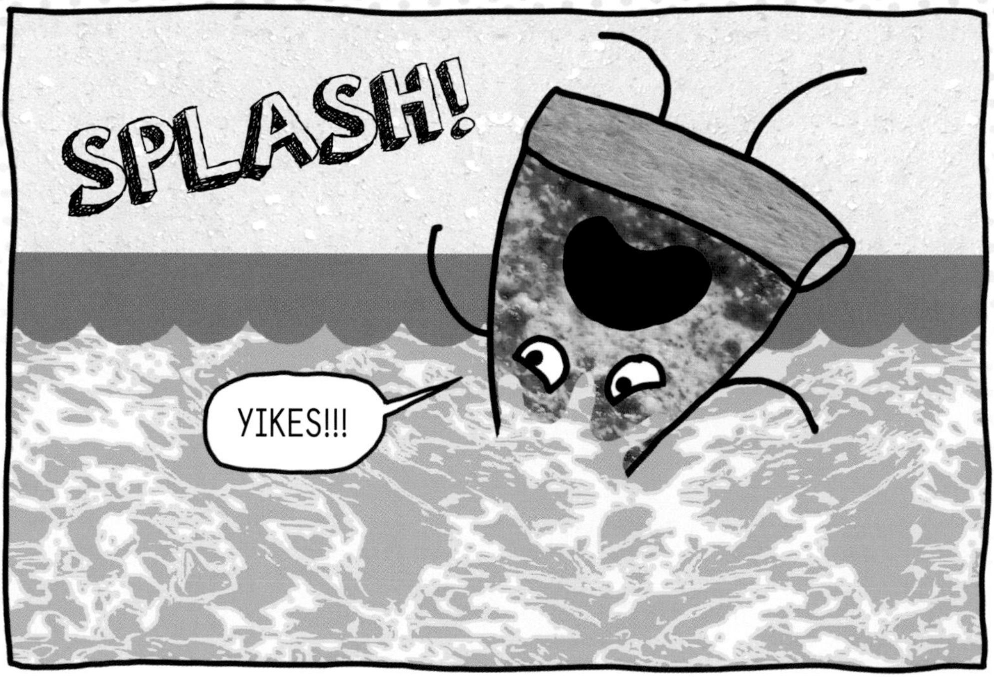
SPLASH!
YIKES!!!

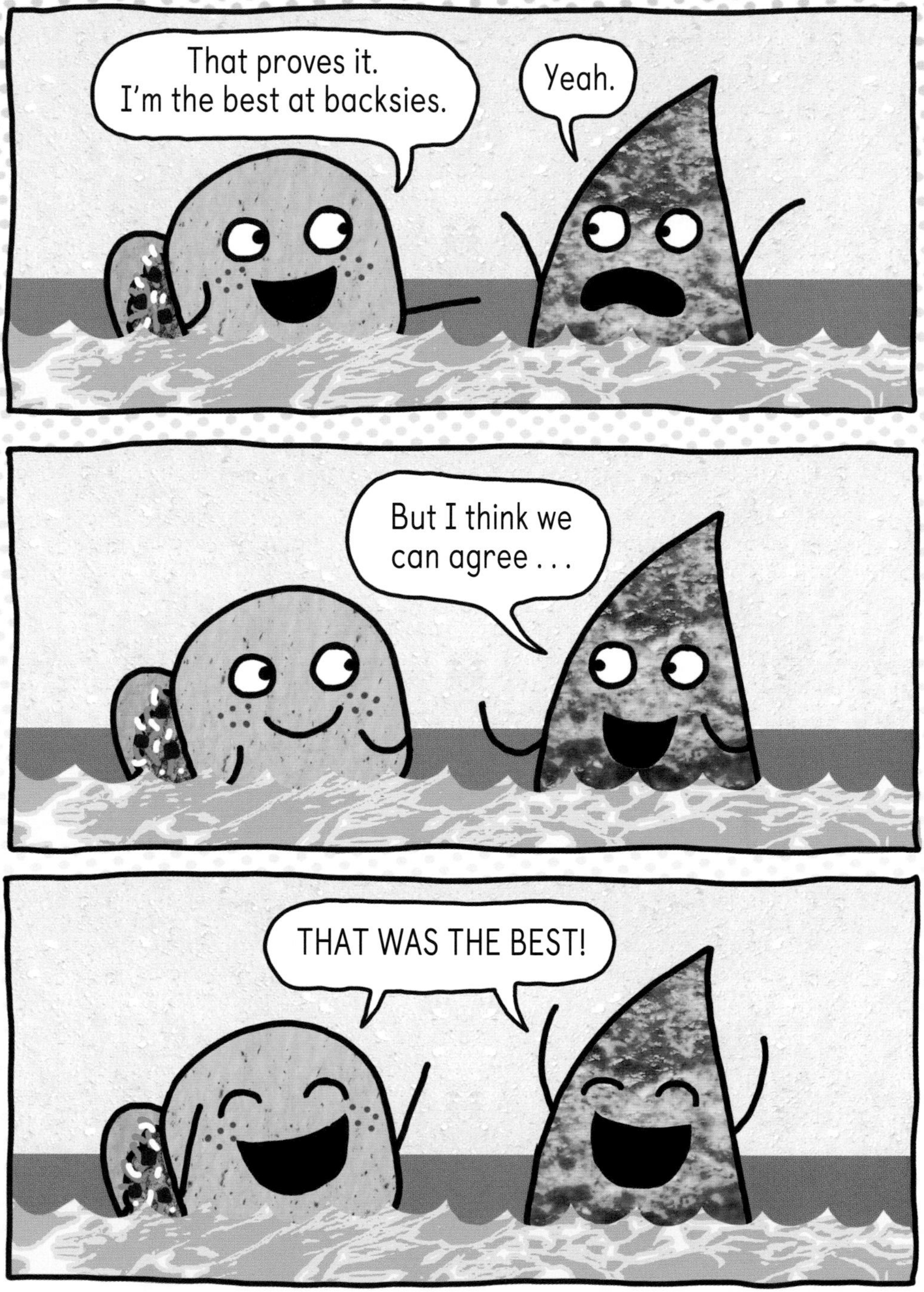
That proves it. I'm the best at backsies.
Yeah.
But I think we can agree . . .
THAT WAS THE BEST!

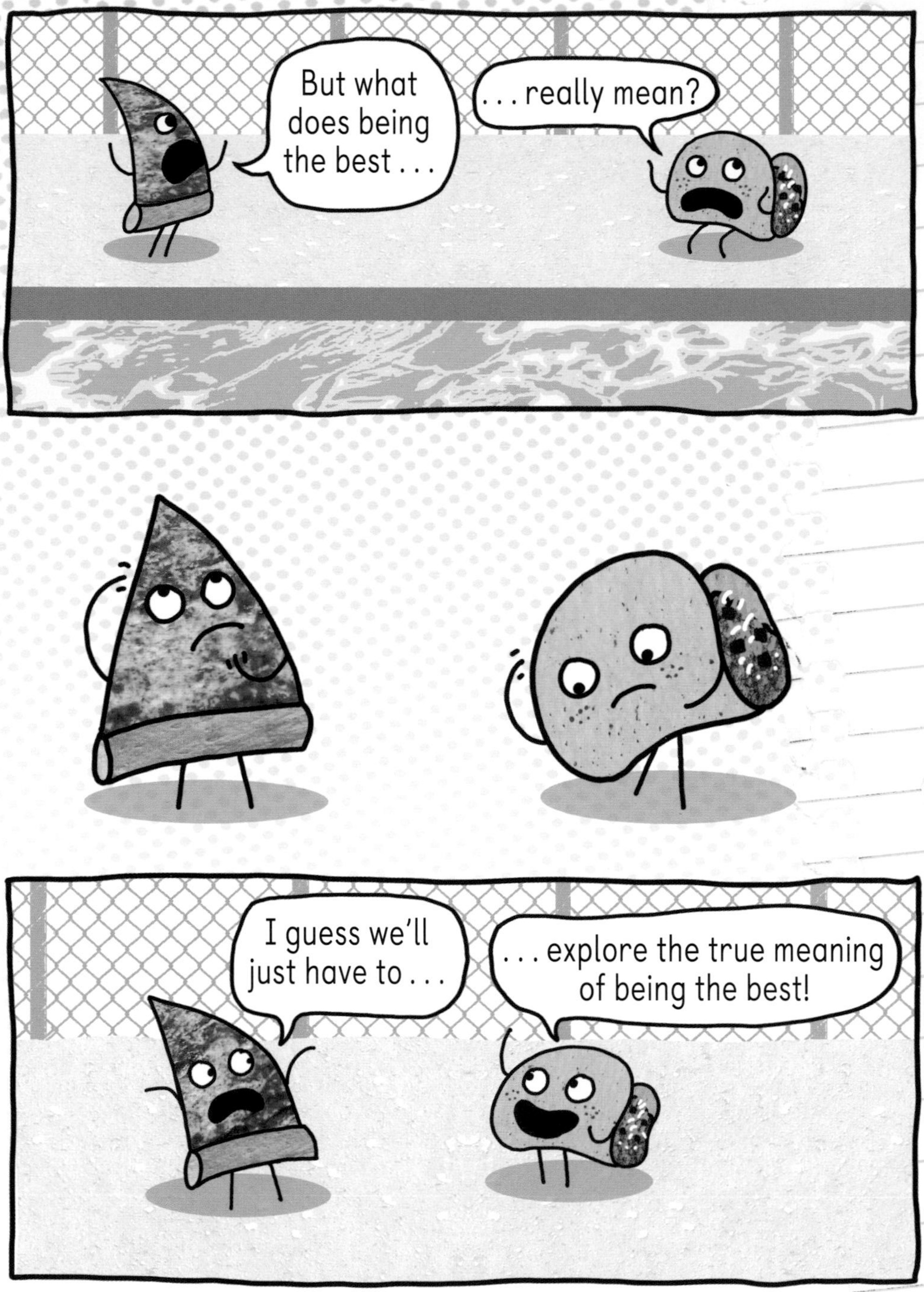
But what does being the best . . .
. . . really mean?
I guess we'll just have to . . .
. . . explore the true meaning of being the best!

Chapter 5
PIZZA and TACO: The True Meaning of Being the Best

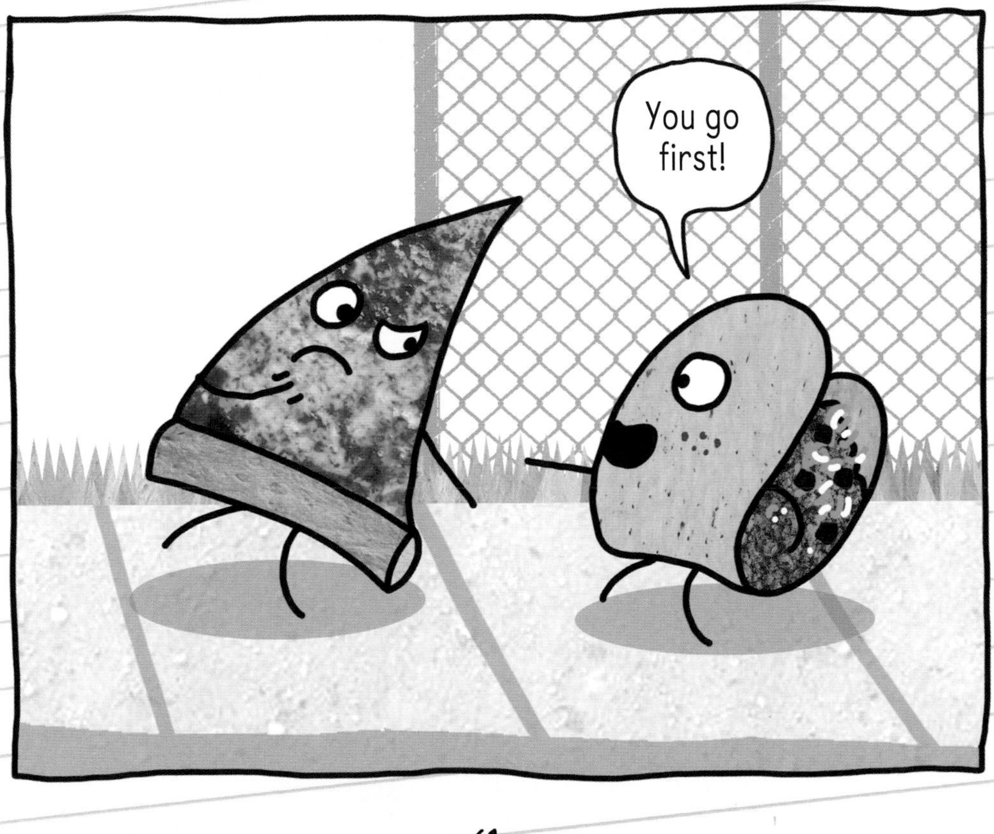
You go first!

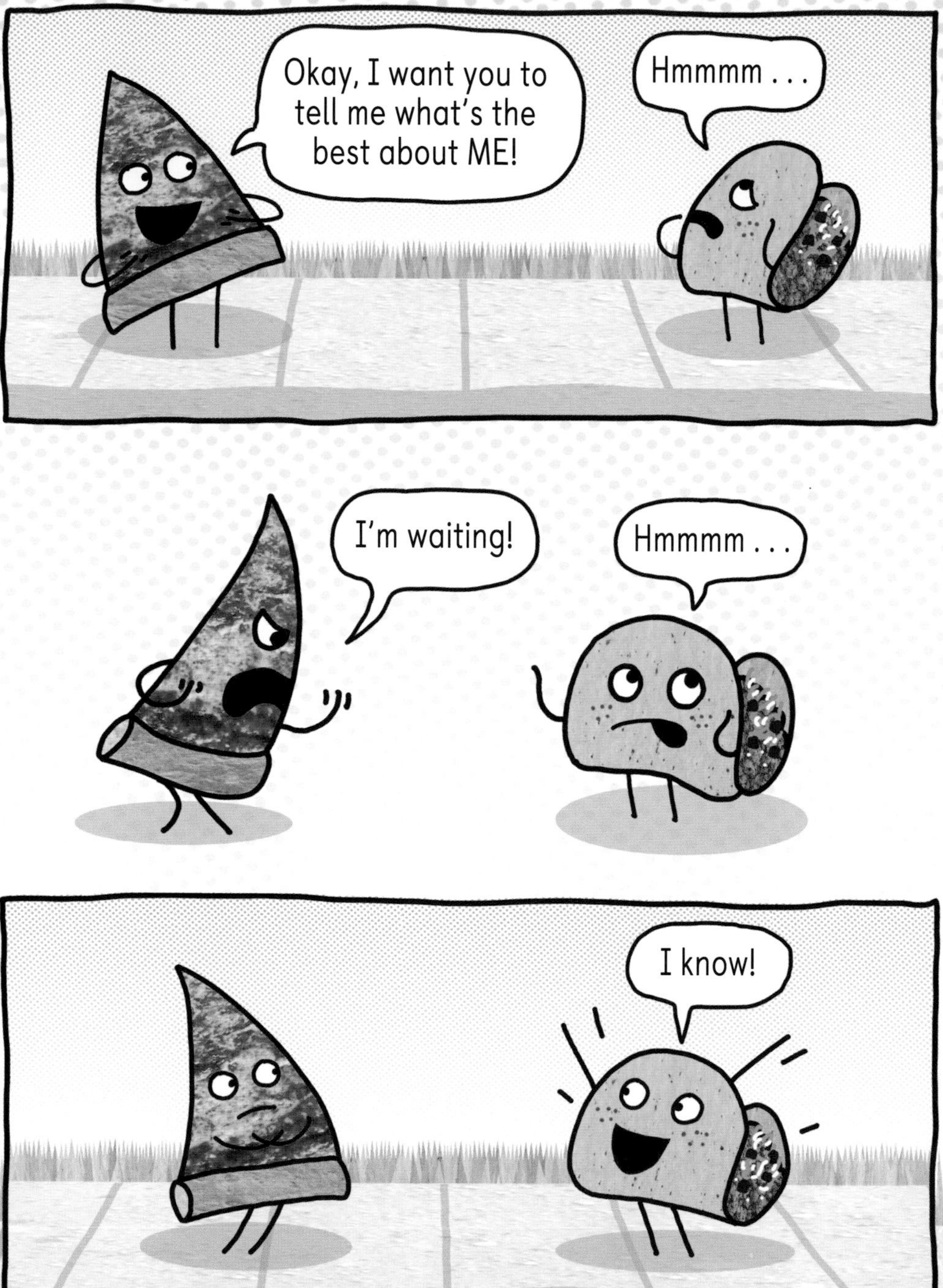
Okay, I want you to tell me what's the best about ME!
Hmmmm . . .
I'm waiting!
Hmmmm . . .
I know!

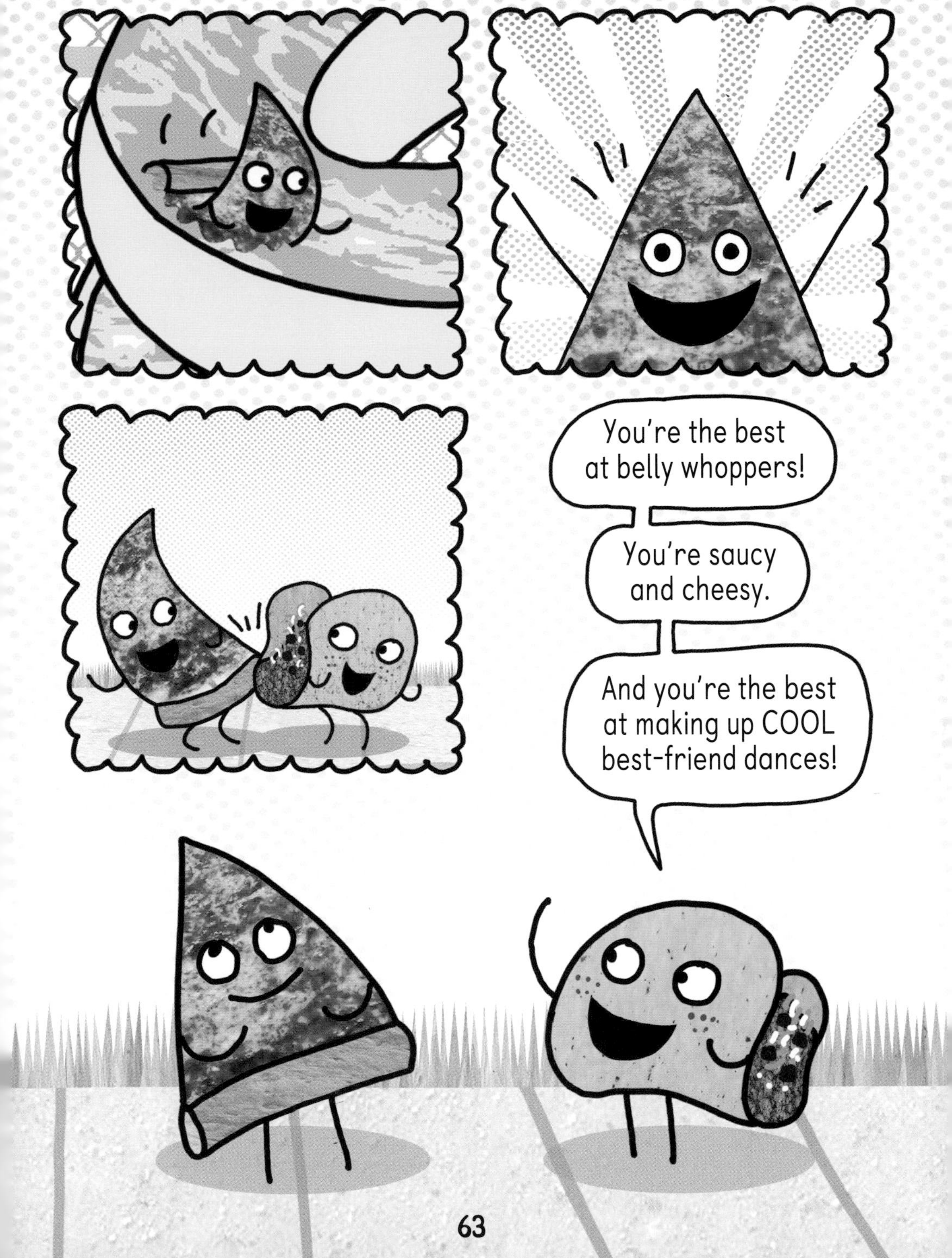
You're the best at belly whoppers!
You're saucy and cheesy.
And you're the best at making up COOL best-friend dances!

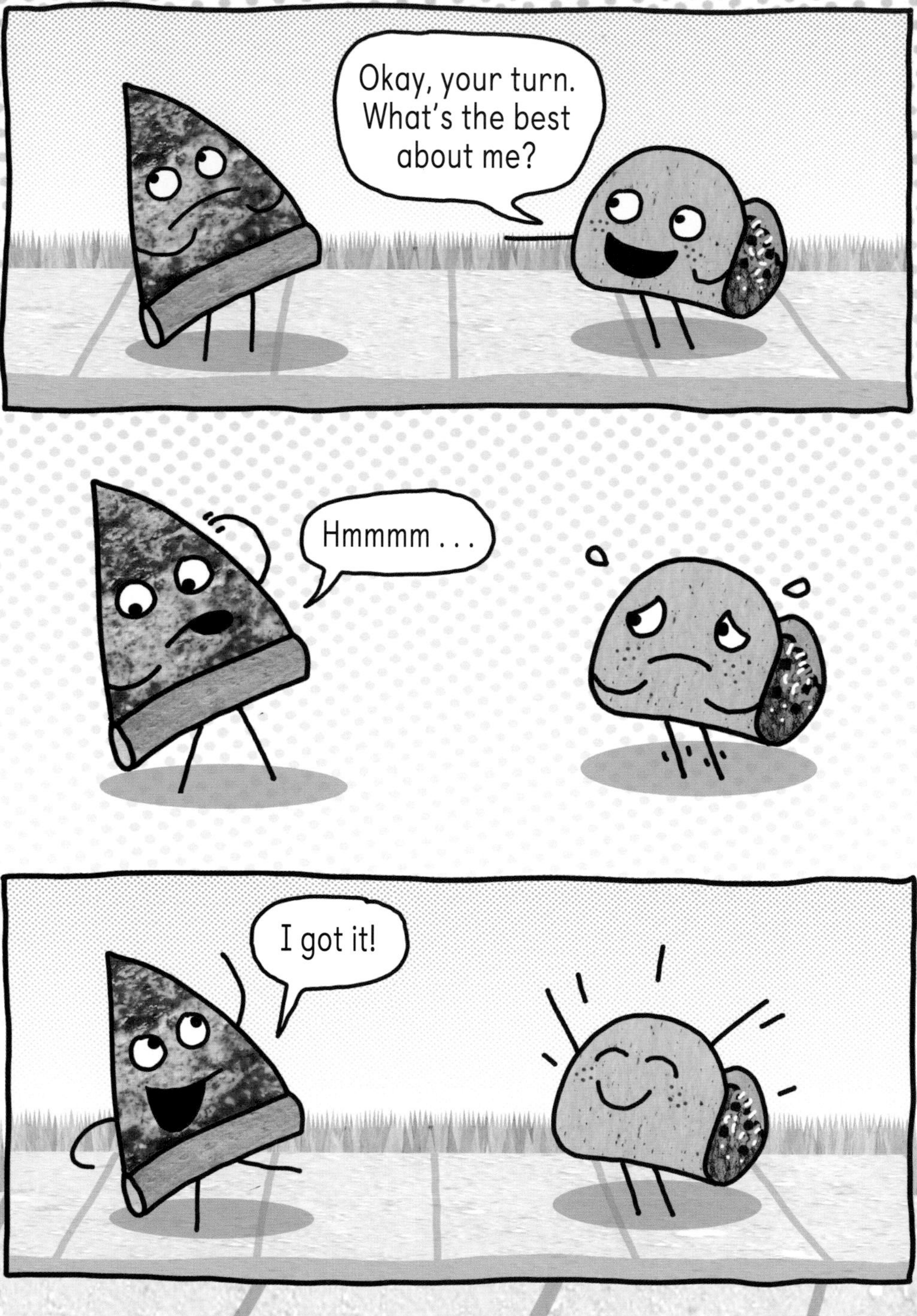
Okay, your turn. What's the best about me?
Hmmmm . . .
I got it!

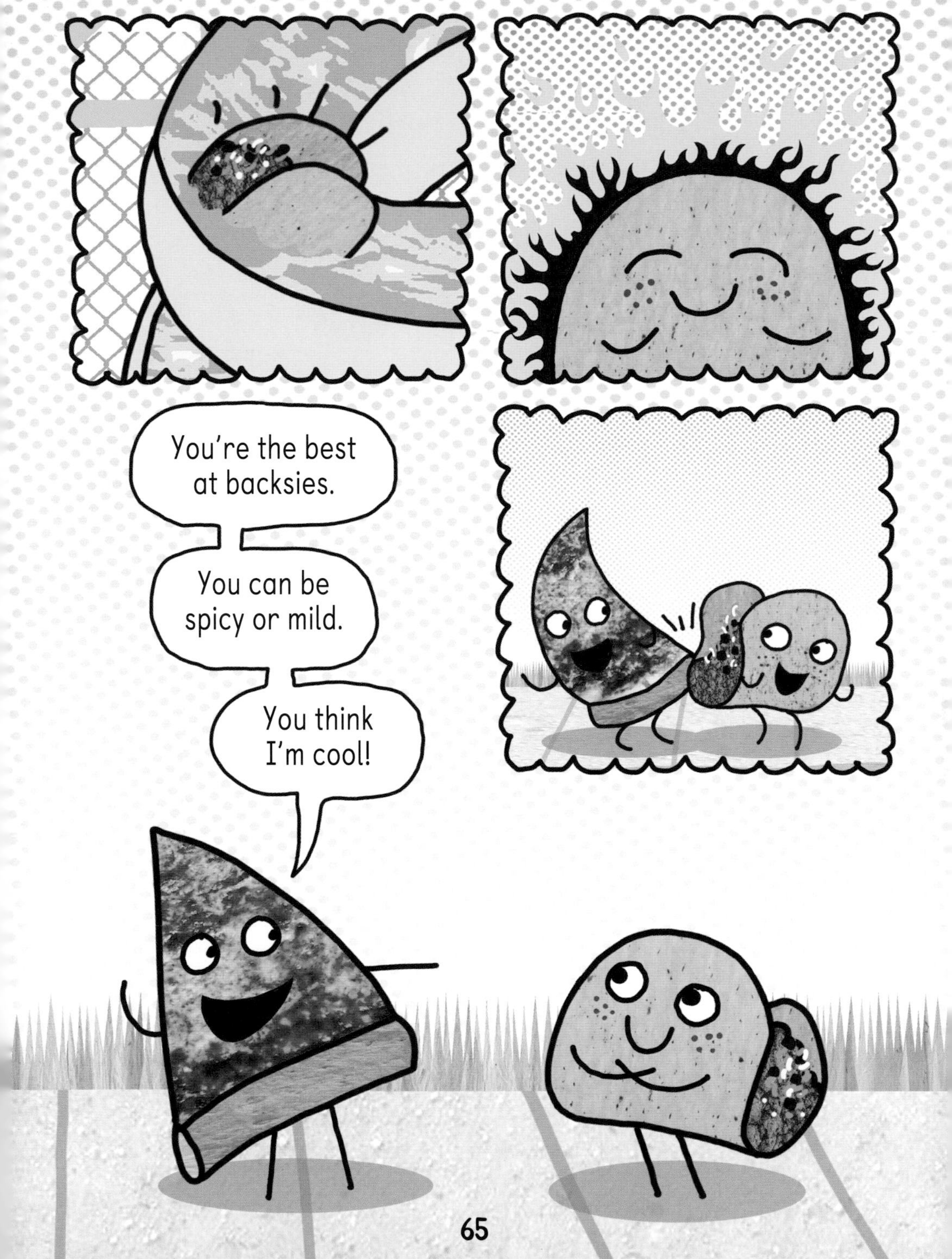
You're the best at backsies.
You can be spicy or mild.
You think I'm cool!

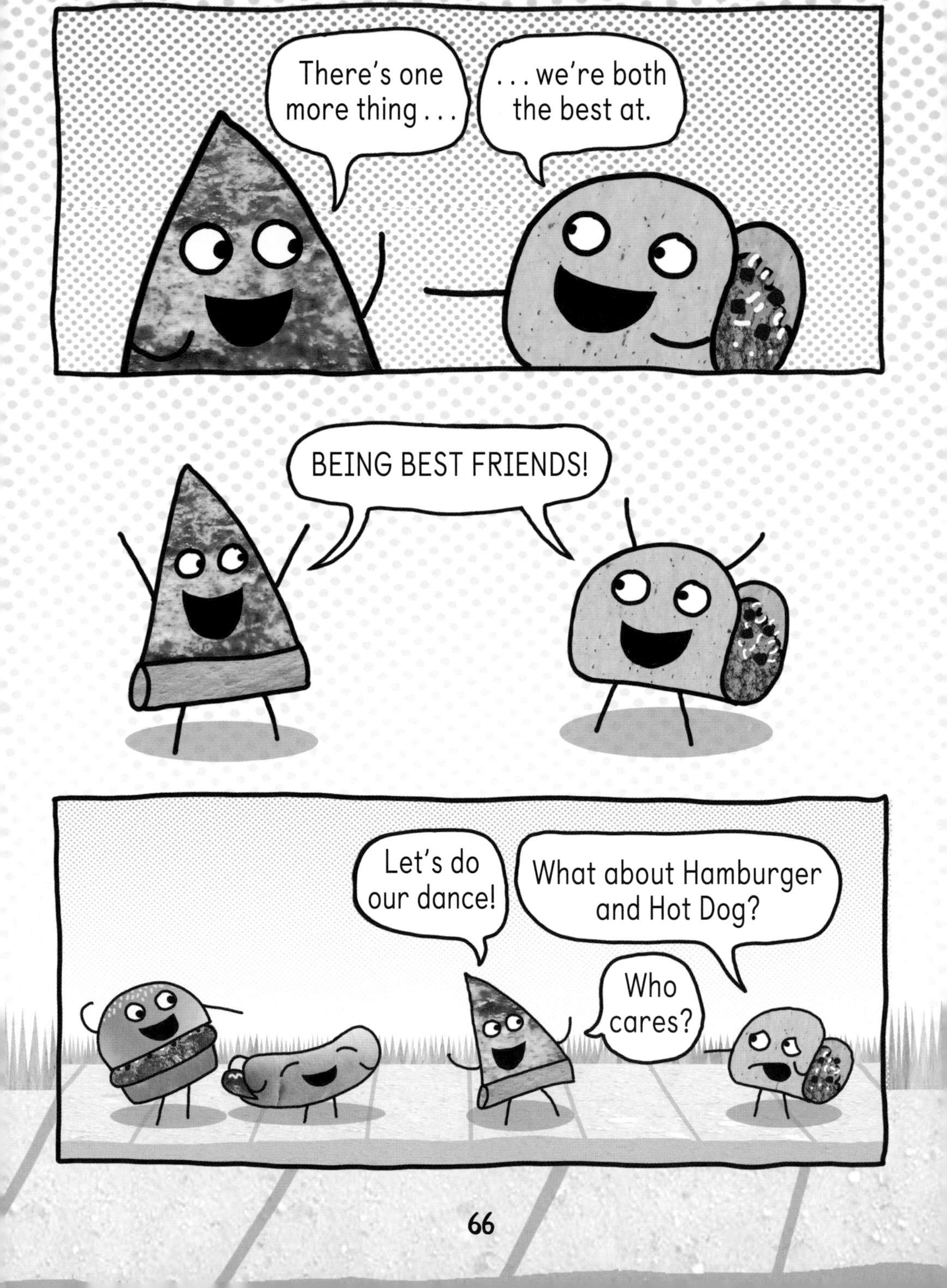
There's one more thing . . .
. . . we're both the best at.
BEING BEST FRIENDS!
Let's do our dance!
What about Hamburger and Hot Dog?
Who cares?

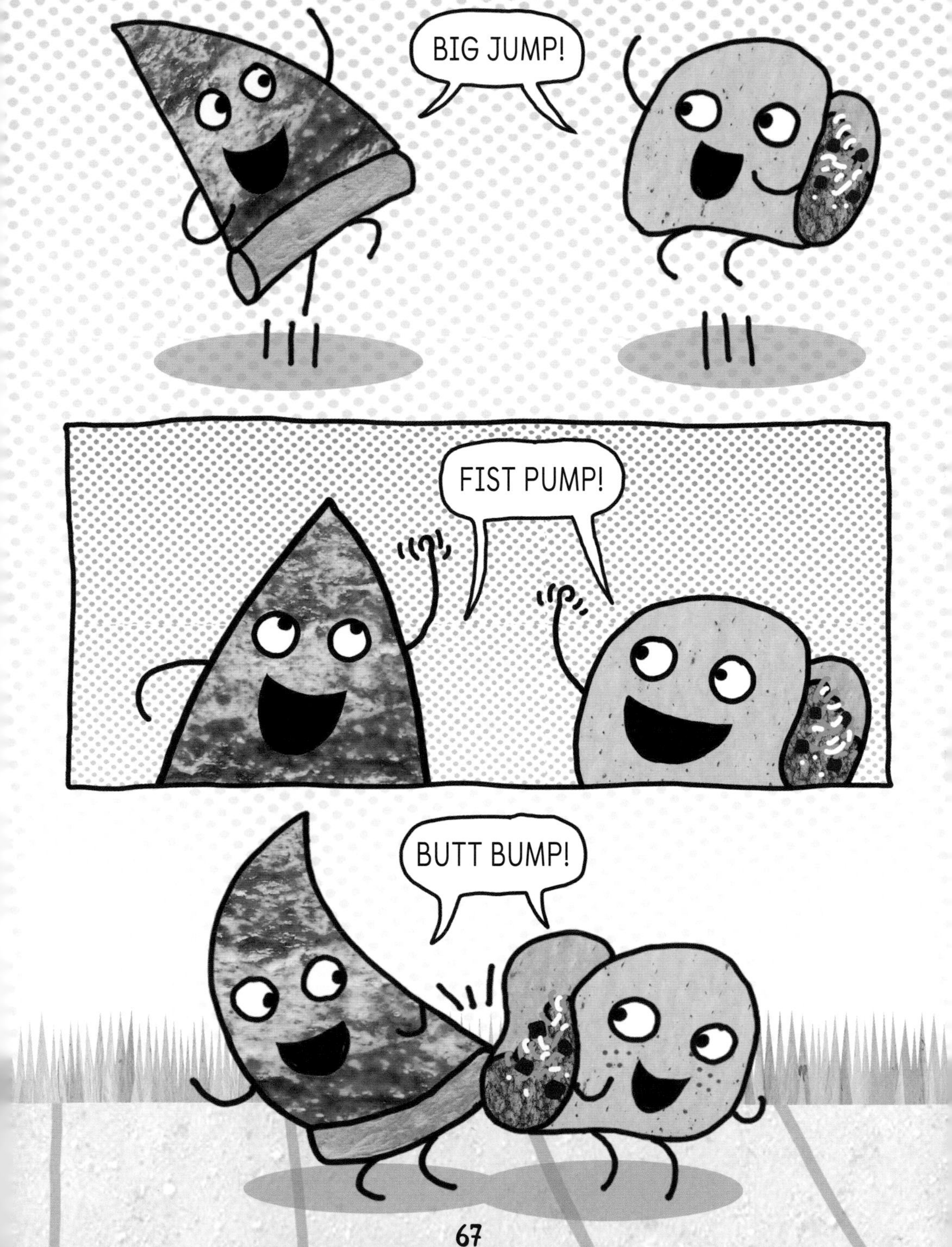
BIG JUMP!
FIST PUMP!
BUTT BUMP!

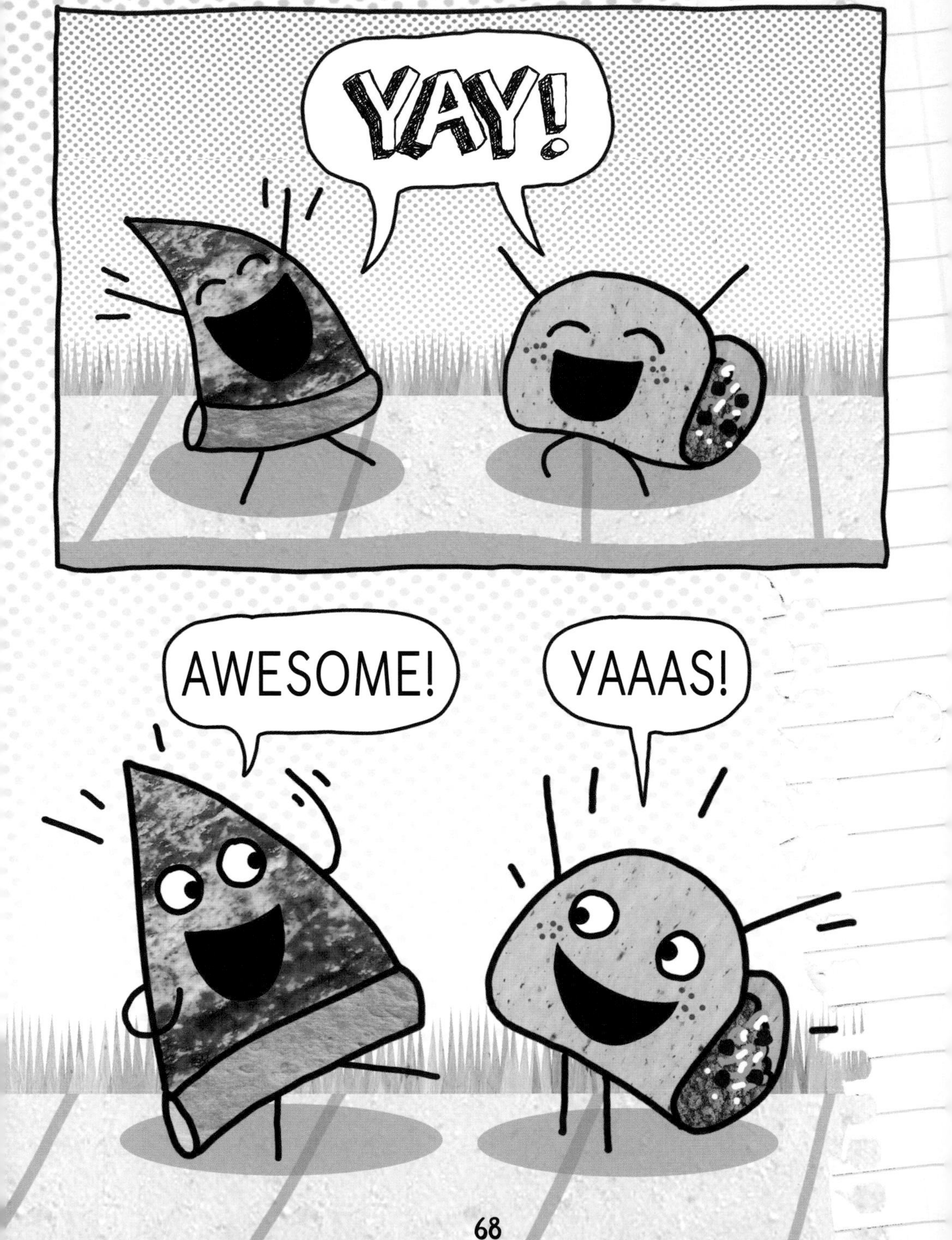
YAY!
AWESOME!
YAAAS!